Where Hope Blooms

DeAnna Julie Dodson

AnniesFiction.com

Books in the Inn at Magnolia Harbor series

Where Hope Blooms
Safe Harbor
Tender Courage

. . . and more to come!

Where Hope Blooms

Library of Congress-in-Publication Data
Where Hope Blooms / by DeAnna Julie Dodson
p. cm.
I. Title
2018957191

AnniesFiction.com
(800) 282-6643
The Inn at Magnolia Harbor™
Series Creator: Shari Lohner
Editor: Shari Lohner
Cover Illustrator: Bonnie Leick

10 11 12 13 14 | Printed in China | 9 8 7 6 5 4 3 2

Grace

"I love it when honeymooners come to stay with us at the inn."

Grace Porter smoothed the downy cream-colored comforter on the king-size four-poster bed and then turned to survey the rest of the Dogwood Suite. The room was large and airy, as classic as the rest of the 1816 mansion that was now Magnolia Harbor Inn, but updated along with the rest of the interior to give it a spacious and luxurious feel. The twin sets of French windows that led out onto the wraparound veranda and overlooked crystal-blue Lake Haven added to the serene beauty of the room. She'd enjoyed her career in marketing, but every day she was grateful that she'd left it to run the inn with her sister.

"This suite is so welcoming and peaceful," she said as she put a piece of gourmet chocolate wrapped in gold foil on each pillow. "I'm sure the bride will love it."

Charlotte Wylde gave her a wry smile as she artfully draped a cozy lavender afghan over one of the overstuffed chairs that stood in front of the unlit fireplace. With her blonde hair and brown eyes—so different from Grace's dark hair and blue eyes—people sometimes didn't realize the two of them were sisters. "If she actually managed to find a decent guy, then all the rest is icing on the cake."

"There are good ones out there." Grace rearranged the white roses in their vase on the round mahogany table, enjoying their intoxicating fragrance as she did. "You just have to keep looking. And don't—"

"And don't settle," Charlotte finished for her with a sigh. "I know. I know."

Charlotte was thirty-four, thirteen years younger than Grace, and despite her big heart, pretty face, and slim figure, she had never been married or engaged. Her gourmet cooking had earned her a cookbook-publishing contract but hadn't attracted any soul mates. After having this discussion more than once over the past fifteen years or so, Grace didn't have anything new to add by way of advice. Her own marriage, though cut tragically short more than twenty years ago, had been warm and loving, and they'd been blessed with a son, Jake. Although Grace was more than content with her life here at the inn, she couldn't blame Charlotte for wanting to find a love of her own.

"Patience," Grace told her sister as usual. "It won't be right until the time is right."

She went into the suite's lavish bathroom, checking one last time to see that the whirlpool tub and large walk-in shower were spotless and everything from the large mirrors over the twin vanities to the white-tiled floor was sparkling. She and Charlotte did most of the work at the inn themselves, and keeping it absolutely pristine was a point of pride for them both. Once Grace had fluffed out the smaller vase of roses on the counter and put fresh bars of handmade lavender-and-frankincense soap in the holders, she returned to the bedroom.

Charlotte stood in the middle of the room, hands on hips, lips thoughtfully pursed. "What do you think? Is it ready?"

Grace studied the room. Then she closed her eyes and drew in a slow, deep breath. The room smelled clean but not in a chemical way, pleasant but not perfumed. Fresh. "I think it's perfect."

Charlotte still frowned. "Too bad it's not cool enough to light a fire. They're always so romantic."

"I suppose there could be a cold snap, but that's not very likely for April in South Carolina. It's forecasted to be in the seventies most days this week. That will be good if our happy newlyweds want to go out on the lake and that sort of thing."

"True," Charlotte said, smiling at last. "And if they—"

The sound of the bell above the front door and Winston's barking cut her off.

"That's either the honeymooners or our Buttercup Suite guest," Grace said. "You'd better make sure everything is shipshape in there, and I'll go see who it is."

Grace made her way to the hallway that overlooked the two-story foyer below and was met by Winston, the inn's little shih tzu mix rescue dog, who was always excited to help welcome guests. He barked and wriggled, his black button eyes shining as she approached him.

"I know it's exciting," she said, leaning down to stroke his glossy brown fur. "I know. Now let's go see who it is." With one hand on the intricately detailed iron railing, she hurried down the curving stairway to the foyer.

Waiting at the front desk was a woman who looked to be thirty or so, tall and athletically built, her smooth caramel-colored skin a lovely contrast to her ivory silk blouse, and her dark curly hair a becoming frame for her sweet face. *Sweet and troubled*, Grace thought as she got closer and saw the woman's eyes.

"Welcome to Magnolia Harbor Inn," she said, and she patted the dog once more. "I'm Grace Porter, and this is Winston. He loves to meet new people."

The other woman smiled tentatively, the eyes behind her glasses dark, long-lashed, and uncertain. "We had a dog like that when I was growing up. It's kind of nice to see one here." She leaned down and cupped Winston's face, her smile warming. "You wouldn't mind playing a little bit sometime, would you?"

Winston yipped and wagged his tail.

"I'm sure that's a no, he wouldn't mind," Grace said. "Why don't we get you checked in, and then you and Winston can make plans."

The woman laughed softly. "I'm Madison Fields. I have a reservation."

"Right. You're here for the reunion."

Madison nodded, her expression darkening once more.

"We've got you in the Buttercup Suite. King-size bed, private bath, claw-foot tub, full lake view, fireplace, and the best service in town."

Madison exhaled heavily. "That will be great."

She didn't at all sound as if it would be great.

"All right," Grace said once she had checked Madison in, "let me show you up to your suite. If you have any special requirements we should be aware of, please let me know. We do our best to accommodate our guests' needs."

Grace grabbed the two largest of the pearl-gray suitcases, and Madison picked up the matching carry-on, accidentally bumping the antique hatbox perched on the corner of the desk. The lid came off when it hit the floor, and several envelopes and folded pieces of paper slid out.

"I'm so sorry." Madison set down her bag and started gathering the papers.

Grace did the same and knelt to help her. "Not a problem."

"What are these?" Madison asked, peering at one of the pages that had fallen open.

Grace caught only a few words before Madison shoved it back into the box with the others: *If you need forgiveness . . .*

"It's kind of a tradition here," Grace said. She took the box from Madison as they stood, put the lid on it and replaced it on the desk. "Sometimes people write down what's troubling them and leave the paper in the box. Sometimes anonymously. Sometimes not."

Madison wrinkled her nose. "What good does that do?"

"People often feel better after they have a chance to get something that's bothering them off their chests without anyone judging them for their feelings or for whatever they might have done."

"And sometimes," said another voice from behind them, "they get answers."

Grace turned, smiling to see her aunt who had come in.

"What are you doing here?" Grace asked, giving her a warm hug as Winston barked and capered around her feet. "Madison, this is my aunt, Winnie Bennett. She lives down the road. Madison is staying with us for her college reunion."

"What fun," Winnie said as she leaned down and picked up the wriggling dog. "I'd hate to tell you how long ago my graduation was."

Madison's shy smile reappeared. "It couldn't have been that long."

"Don't tell anyone," Winnie said in a stage whisper, "but I'm sixty-nine."

"She loves telling people that," Grace said, and there was no reason her aunt shouldn't be pleased to give her real age. Her thick, dark blonde hair held only a hint of gray, and her hazel eyes were always bright. Though she was only five foot three, she was a bundle of energy, fit and active.

"I was taking my morning walk," Winnie said, "and I thought I'd stop by and see what you girls were up to. I'm so glad I got to meet you, Madison. Will you be staying long?"

"Until Sunday," Madison told her. "The reunion dance is Saturday night, and that's the last event. Between now and then we're having a softball game and a picnic and I don't know what else. I think the guys are planning to go see some NASCAR races, but I'll probably pass on that."

"Good. That should give you plenty of time to relax and enjoy yourself at the inn too." Winnie tapped the hatbox with one finger.

"And this is for anyone who wants to use it. No extra charge."

"Thank you. But I think all I need is a little rest. It's been a long day."

"Sounds like a good idea," Winnie said, and then she turned to Grace. "Now, where's your sister? In the kitchen?"

"If she's not still upstairs." Grace picked up Madison's luggage again. "If she is, I'll send her down."

Winnie nodded and carried a squirming Winston toward the kitchen. "Winston and I are helping ourselves to a cold drink."

Grace gave them a fond smile and then led her guest up the stairs.

"It's a beautiful place," Madison said once they were at the top. She gazed down over the white marble foyer. "It looks brand-new inside, but I'm guessing this mansion is at least a hundred years old."

"A little over two hundred, actually," Grace told her. "It was a private home until we bought it seven years ago and did some remodeling and updating. I'd be happy to give you a tour once you're settled in, or feel free to explore on your own. We want our guests to feel at home here and have a place to get away from all the bustle and trouble out in the real world."

Madison didn't reply to that, and the rest of the walk to her room was silent, but once inside she seemed to relax. The Buttercup Suite was painted a soft yellow with white trim, as unpretentious and cozy as its name. It was the perfect getaway.

"Nice," she said as she ran one hand over the cream-and-burgundy toile bedspread. "It feels nice." She gazed around the room. "I love it."

"Wonderful. Now if you need anything at all, you let me know." Grace turned to go and then paused. "I meant to tell you that we have three others who are planning to stay here for your reunion. I'll be happy to introduce you all later if you'd like. You might even know them already."

Madison swallowed hard and then shook her head. "Thank you, but

I'm really tired right now. If you don't mind, I'll just unpack and relax."

"I'm sure you'll have plenty of time to catch up with your classmates later on," Grace said, wondering at the younger woman's reaction. "Don't forget that dinner is on your own, but we serve complimentary wine, cheese, and my sister's delicious hors d'oeuvres between six and seven out on the back veranda. The view is lovely that time of day, and a lot of people enjoy eating out there. Come downstairs if you're interested."

"Thank you," Madison said with her hand already on the door, obviously ready for Grace to leave. "I think I'd rather eat up here tonight, if that's okay. I know you usually only serve breakfast, but I'm seriously exhausted. Would you be willing to send something up? It doesn't have to be anything fancy. A sandwich or something would do. You can put it on my bill."

She did seem tired, but Grace thought it was more than physical.

Grace patted her arm. "We can do that. I'll call you in a little while and tell you what's available, and you can let me know exactly what you'd like."

"Anything, honestly," Madison said. "I'm sure it's all fine. Bring me whatever you have, but nothing too heavy, all right?"

"I'll be happy to. Meanwhile, you make yourself at home."

"Thanks."

Before Grace could say anything more, Madison shut the door. The sound of the dead bolt being turned was unmistakable. Grace had been in the business long enough to know that things weren't as they seemed with Madison. She wasn't simply tired. Something was troubling her, weighing heavy on her heart.

Grace had a feeling things were going to get worse before they got better.

2

Madison

If you need forgiveness . . . Madison couldn't shake the thought of the note she had glimpsed in the hatbox downstairs. *Forgiveness? Ridiculous.* Who looked for forgiveness in a hatbox? And what good would that forgiveness do her when she couldn't begin to forgive herself?

She bustled around the room for a few minutes, unpacking her suitcases and arranging everything in the armoire and in the bathroom. It really was a magnificent room, one she could easily curl up in and never come out of again, but that wasn't what she was here for.

A class reunion should be fun, right? She had been close to Kathy, Emma, and Kim in high school, and then in their sorority days. They were the popular girls, the ones everyone wanted around—bright, involved, stylish, and determined to change the world for good. What wasn't to like? Why wouldn't she want to see them again?

She sighed. Maybe she didn't want them to see her. After all, they probably remembered her as a nice person—someone who played fair and worked hard for everything she got.

Someone who would never deliberately ruin another person's life.

Her shoes were torture, so she kicked them off and then flung herself down on the bed. The headboard and footboard were made of carved dark wood, rich and highly polished, as stylish and luxurious as everything else in the room. She closed her eyes and let herself sink into the downy bedding. If only she could stay right where she was until the reunion was over.

That was a silly thought. She turned over and buried her head under the pillow, but even then it was too light to sleep and she wasn't tired. Not that kind of tired, anyway. Still, she knew she'd never actually get to sleep. She shouldn't have come. She had never forgotten what she'd done, but for long stretches of time she had managed to push it to the back of her mind. Had she expected to come to her reunion and not drown in the memory? She'd graduated with honors and quickly found a high-paying job. No one looking at her home or her clothes or her car could deny that the past ten years of her life had been a great success. But they couldn't see her heart. They didn't know that everything she had, everything she was, was because of her selfishness and spite. Because of her cowardice.

If you need forgiveness . . .

She turned over again and lay sprawled on her back, her head on the pillow rather than under it, then rolled to her other side. There was a large flat-screen TV on the dresser, but somehow the thought of watching it didn't appeal to her. Neither did reading any of the books she had in her carry-on. The only thing she wanted to do was dig in that hatbox and see what kinds of notes other people had written. What had they wanted advice about, and had anyone answered them?

If you need forgiveness . . .

It was a ridiculous thought, but what would it hurt after all? Grace had said that some people felt better simply getting their troubles off their minds and onto paper. Madison climbed out of bed and went to the secretary desk in the corner. As she'd expected, she found pens and pencils and some nice stationery inside. She pulled up the chair and sat down.

Fifteen years ago—

She slashed through the words. It didn't matter how long it had been, though she was a little startled to realize it had been that long now. Nearly half her lifetime. Too long to have carried this inside her.

One spiteful act had changed the course of a life, a life she had considered to be less important than her own. After all, it was only Poor Marvin . . .

I messed up, she wrote. *I didn't think it would turn out the way it did, and then I was too afraid to make it right. I would have had to leave school, and Mom and Dad would have been so disappointed in me. I wanted to make them proud.*

No, that wasn't true. Okay, yes, she had wanted to make them proud, but their disappointment hadn't been why she'd hidden what she'd done. It was time she was honest, even if it was only with an old hatbox.

More than that, though, I didn't want to be embarrassed in front of everybody. I didn't want people to ~~think~~ know I was petty and thoughtless. I didn't want them to ~~think~~ know I was capable of something like that. I was an honor student—smart, talented, destined for success. Not like Poor Marvin.

They'd always called him Poor Marvin, as if that were his name. No doubt her Aunt Ruby from Georgia would have added "bless his heart."

After I heard what happened to his mother, I wanted to tell him what I did and beg him to forgive me. I even bought a sympathy card and wrote a long note inside it, but then I tore it up and threw it away. What good would it have done him? Didn't he have enough to deal with? After that, I convinced myself that it was better not to say anything. Why should I stir up old hurts just to make myself feel better?

But I knew the real question was deeper than that: Why should I make myself vulnerable when he might reject my apology? When I might have to hear firsthand how my cruelty had affected him? I want to think I've grown up enough to face what I've done. I want to think that even if he does reject me, even if he has carried nothing but hatred for me all these years, I am strong enough to do the right thing.

I want so much to be done with this. Even if it's painful, I want to end it once and for all. I want him to know I never thought what I did would hurt him so badly. I want to say I'm sorry.

I don't know if I can.

She blinked back tears as she folded the note.

She hadn't signed it, but that didn't matter. Nobody was likely to read it anyway.

After a few minutes, she unfolded it and read it again. Then she dropped it into the trash can next to the desk and walked over to the French windows. It was a gorgeous view. It would be nice to sit out on the dock and think. Or maybe not. It didn't do any good to think if she never figured out a way to make things right.

She fished the note out of the trash and went downstairs.

3

Grace

Once she left the Buttercup Suite, Grace made a beeline to the kitchen. Charlotte and Winnie were sitting at the big marble-topped island in the middle of the room, drinking tall glasses of iced tea while Winston dozed at their feet. Despite its generous size, large windows, and light coloring that made it feel even larger, the kitchen was always warm and welcoming.

"There you are," Winnie said, and she pushed a glass of tea toward Grace. "Come sit down with us."

"Only for a minute," Grace said. "I have to make sure the rest of the rooms are tidied up before our other guests arrive."

"I already straightened the Wisteria Loft Suite," Charlotte told her, "so that leaves Bluebell and Rosebud. It's nice to have a full house."

"It's nice to have that reunion bringing people in." Grace sipped her tea and then glanced up toward the second floor. "Oh, by the way, we'll need a sandwich or something sent up for dinner to the Buttercup Suite. Madison said whatever you fix will be fine, as long as it's not heavy."

"Okay." Charlotte gave her a questioning look. "Winnie says that one has a lot on her mind."

Grace nodded. "She's here for the reunion, but I'm not sure if she's going to do anything but hide out in her room until she leaves on Sunday."

"Maybe peace and quiet is what she really needs," Winnie said with a sympathetic smile. "And if that's the case, she's picked the perfect place to find it."

"It seems odd that she would come at all if that's how she feels," Charlotte said. "But perhaps she's simply tired, like she said. I always forget how traveling takes it out of you. And I bet she won't be the only one coming to the reunion with some nerves and insecurities haunting her."

Grace laughed softly. "True enough. You wouldn't think she'd have much of anything to worry about. She looks as if she's been very successful since she got out of school."

"Looks can be deceiving," Winnie said.

Charlotte pursed her lips. "Tell me about it."

Grace and Winnie exchanged a glance.

"I guess The Tidewater is full up this week too," Grace said.

Charlotte scowled at her. "I'm sure it is. And I'm sure Dean will be delighted to serve his guests all the recipes he stole from me."

"Now, Charlotte," Winnie began, but Charlotte cut her off.

"No. I said 'stole' and that's what I meant. I don't care if I don't have proof that would stand up in a court of law. I know. Just like I know he was only pretending to care about me so he could steal them."

"Yes," Grace said mildly, "because nobody could possibly be interested in you for yourself."

Charlotte huffed. "Dean Bradley is a snake. You know he opened The Tidewater on the other side of the lake to annoy me."

"That's a pretty elaborate plan merely to annoy someone," Winnie observed.

"I'm sure it's all very funny to both of you," Charlotte said primly. "Grace at least had a husband, and you've been married to Uncle Gus for over fifty years now. You don't know how it is."

"You're right, honey." Winnie gave Charlotte's shoulders a

squeeze. "We don't know exactly how it is for you to not have found the right guy yet, but don't you think you're giving Dean a little too much consideration? If he's as awful as you say, why waste your time thinking of him?"

Charlotte crossed her arms over her chest. "He's proof that most of the good ones are taken and only the jerks are left."

"I know you don't really believe that," Grace said.

Charlotte waved a dismissive hand. "He can do what he wants. I've already made arrangements."

Grace's eyebrows went up. "Arrangements?"

"You may as well know now. I've hired a professional matchmaker."

Winnie laughed and then abruptly cleared her throat. "A matchmaker?"

Charlotte nodded defiantly. "I decided it was time I took a more practical approach to dating. A matchmaker will find me someone who's actually suited to me, someone who's serious about settling down. I'm not getting any younger, you know."

"I see," Winnie said with a glance at Grace. "That should be interesting."

"I don't know what it could hurt." Grace gave her sister a warm smile. "In fact, it might be a lot of fun. But make sure you meet whoever they match you with in a safe place."

"I know," Charlotte said, a glimmer of excitement showing in her dark eyes. "The matchmaker went over all that with me. It's very carefully planned. We'll meet in a restaurant at a busy time, and I don't even have to tell my date anything but my first name if I don't want to. That way if he turns out to be a creep, he doesn't have any way to get in touch with me again."

"I bet it'll be fun," Winnie said, clearly warming up to the idea. "And who knows? Maybe you'll actually find Mr. Right."

"Or at least meet a nice guy," Grace added. "And, as you say, someone who's serious about settling down."

Before Charlotte could reply, a loud knock sounded. Winston was awake and at the kitchen door when it opened and Spencer Lewis leaned in.

"Are we interrupting?"

The other half of "we" was the chocolate lab that had wriggled her way inside in order to exchange nose rubs with Winston and then help herself to his water bowl.

"Come in." Grace got up and opened the door wide. "We were having some iced tea. Would you like a glass?"

"That'd be great." Spencer blotted his face on the sleeve of his sweatshirt and then ran one hand through his short salt-and-pepper hair. "Please excuse how I look. Bailey and I just took a jog into town." He sat next to Charlotte and put a paper bag on the island. "I thought I'd stop by and drop these off."

"Oooh, is that what I think it is?" Charlotte opened the bag and smiled. "Wonderful! Now I can make the chocolate pecan pie I've been dying to try. Thank you for picking them up for me. What do we owe you?"

"Not a thing." He smiled at Grace, his blue eyes crinkling at the corners. "But I want you both to remember that when Blossom Hill Farm has its own crop of pecans this fall, we'd sure like to be the inn's main supplier."

"It's a deal," Grace said, returning his smile.

Even sweaty and rumpled, he was an attractive man. At fifty, he was tall and lean, quick to smile but calm and deliberate too—qualities that had no doubt served him well during his long career with the FBI.

"How are things going out at the farm?" Winnie asked. "All settled in?"

"Not bad for less than a month," Spencer told her. "Bailey and I have things pretty much on track, though there's no way to make pecans ripen before they're ready. Still, after all my years with the Bureau, it's good to start fresh and not have to worry about anything but my own little plot of ground and how to make it bloom. Early retirement is treating me well."

Winnie beamed at him. "I'm glad you're so close to the inn. With my place a short walk down the road the other way, I don't have to worry about the girls."

Charlotte rolled her eyes, and Grace laughed.

"You certainly don't," Spencer said gallantly. "I hope they know they can call on me any time they need something."

"I promise we won't take advantage of your generosity," Grace told him.

He gave her a smile. "I'm sorry to hear that."

Before Grace could formulate a reply, both dogs started barking. A second later, the front bell rang.

Spencer grabbed Bailey's collar when she tried to take off behind Winston. "I think we'd better get going. Sounds like you're about to be busy."

"I'll bet that's our blissful couple, ready to start their honeymoon," Grace said, hurrying after her own dog. "See you later."

The woman standing at the desk was in her early thirties, her pretty face framed by light brown hair with a few sun streaks. Clad in a flowing sundress and sandals, she appeared ready to relax and enjoy her honeymoon. But as Grace drew nearer, she caught a hard glint in the woman's hazel eyes and knew something wasn't right—something that probably meant trouble for whomever the woman had on her mind.

"Good afternoon," Grace said, giving her best smile. "How may I help you?"

The woman dumped her shoulder bag onto the front desk, her mouth a tight line. "I have a reservation for the week. The Dogwood Suite."

"Oh, yes. Mrs. Sarah Nicholson. Best wishes to you and your new husband, and welcome to Magnolia Harbor Inn."

The woman's frown deepened. "No, it's O'Donnell. *Miss* O'Donnell. And it's probably never going to be anything different."

"But Mr. Nicholson—"

"Mr. Nicholson," the woman said, lifting her chin as her eyes flashed, "has made other plans."

Charlotte poked her head out the kitchen door. She caught Grace's eye and raised an eyebrow.

Grace understood her sister's unspoken question. Could a stay at the inn work its magic on these troubled guests as it had so many before and help them find the healing they needed?

Grace gave a small nod in reply. It was time to get to work.

Grace

Grace bit her lip, not wanting to say the wrong thing to this obviously hurting woman. "I hope everything's all right."

"Everything's absolutely fabulous. Couldn't be better." Sarah O'Donnell gave her a fierce smile. "I didn't end up marrying the biggest jerk in the whole world after all, so yippee, right?"

Grace couldn't help wincing slightly. "I'm sorry."

"Don't be. We may have had to cancel the wedding, but the reception was already paid for, so I wasn't about to miss that." Sarah lifted her chin. "Best party I ever went to."

"I, uh—"

"And now I'm going to have the loveliest honeymoon any groomless bride ever had."

Grace nodded. "Your room—"

"It's supposed to be paid for already. Or did the jerk back out on that too?"

"No, no. Everything's ready for your stay. I was only going to say that I'll be happy to show you up."

Sarah shouldered her bag again and bent to pick up the obviously new designer suitcase she had carried in.

"Let me get that." Grace hurried around to the other side of the desk. But before she reached Sarah's side, the front bell rang again.

The man who walked in wore jeans and a T-shirt with a jacket tossed over his shoulder, and was pulling a large black suitcase behind him. He looked Sarah up and down from behind his sunglasses and then pushed the glasses up into his spiked sandy hair.

"Hi," he said. "Are you here for the reunion?"

Sarah's mouth was set in a tight line. "No."

"I didn't think so. I'm sure I would have remembered you if we'd been at school together." He glanced at Grace. "Keith Chastain. I have a reservation." Before Grace could say a word, he turned back to Sarah. "You know, a lot of the events are open to alumni and their guests." He gave her a slow grin. "If you're at loose ends, I'd be happy to let you tag along."

Sarah's mouth tightened even more.

"I'm sorry to interrupt, Mr. Chastain," Grace said with a professional smile, "but I need to show this guest up to her room. I'll have my sister come and get you checked in and see to everything you need."

Keith shrugged and leaned on the desk. "No hurry. Hey, has Mike checked in yet? Mike Mitchell. He and I roomed together back in the day."

"Not yet," Grace told him. "But we're expecting him any minute. Oh, here's my sister."

Charlotte hurried out of the kitchen. "I heard the bell and thought you could use some help."

"Right on time." Grace flashed her a grateful smile. "Mr. Chastain would like to check in. He's in the Rosebud Suite."

Keith stood up straight. "Aw, you're kidding me, right? Rosebud?"

"All of our rooms are named after flowers," Grace explained.

"I think it's charming," Sarah said, with only the slightest bit of hauteur in her tone.

"Well, yeah, sure," Keith said. "But don't you have one called 'Titan' or 'Avenger' or something like that?" He glanced at Sarah out of the corner of his eye. "Or how about the 'Super Cool Guy Suite'?"

For the first time, Sarah cracked a small but genuine smile.

"We'll take that under consideration," Grace assured him, and then she picked up Sarah's suitcase. "If you'd like to follow me, I'll show you to your room. Charlotte will take care of you, Mr. Chastain."

"See you around," Keith said as Sarah followed Grace up the stairs. "I'll be here all week."

Sarah was silent until she and Grace were in the Dogwood Suite.

"This is nice," she said finally, and she walked to the windows to gaze out over Lake Haven. "It's really pretty."

"Wait until you see it at sunset." Grace put down the suitcase and came to stand beside her. This was a sight she never tired of. "There are such gorgeous colors shimmering on the surface of the water."

"Yeah. Until it turns black when night falls."

Grace didn't reply, though she raised a quick prayer for wisdom. What could she say that would soothe rather than irritate?

"You don't do dinner, right?" Sarah asked.

"We don't usually, but we can certainly make something for you if you don't feel like going out this evening. You're also welcome to help yourself to the complimentary wine, cheese, and hors d'oeuvres we offer from six until seven every evening. We usually serve it all on the back veranda overlooking the lake, and of course, the view is gorgeous from there too. If you'd rather, I can tell you about some lovely local restaurants. If you like steak and seafood, Turner's—"

"No. I only asked because I didn't want you fixing anything for me tonight. I couldn't eat it."

"I understand. But if you change your mind, let me know. My sister is a great cook, and she could whip up something for you in a jiffy."

"Thank you," Sarah said. "That's very kind of you and her, but I'm fine right now. I think I'll get a good night's sleep and then figure out tomorrow what I'm going to do."

She glanced over at the bed, the four-poster bed with its cream-colored linens and the twin pieces of foil-wrapped chocolate on the plump pillows, and her eyes filled with tears. Grace wanted so much to put her arms around her and let her cry out all the ache in her heart, but Sarah seemed too defensive right now to accept comfort from anyone, especially a total stranger. Grace had to settle for a sympathetic smile.

"I think that's a great idea. Rest tonight and let tomorrow take care of itself. A lot of people come here when they need a place to relax and get away from everything. I know this visit isn't what you had originally planned, but maybe this is exactly the right place for you all the same. Things always look better in the morning."

Sarah's face hardened. "I know you mean well," she said, "and I appreciate your kindness, but I'm perfectly fine. None of this is going to be better in the morning, or in a whole lot of mornings. I have to learn to deal with it and never let myself be so stupid again." She finally met Grace's gaze, her fierce smile firmly in place. "Besides, I'm here to have the time of my life."

Grace nodded. "If there's anything at all that you'd like, please let me know." As much as she would have liked to offer more words of comfort, it was obvious that Sarah wasn't ready to hear them.

She stepped into the hallway and shut the door to the Dogwood Suite quietly behind her.

That evening, Grace carried a tray up to the Buttercup Suite and tapped on the door.

After a long moment, the door opened. Madison had clearly just woken up, judging by her rumpled clothes, no makeup, and her springy curls in a wild tangle. She blinked at Grace as if she couldn't quite recognize the innkeeper without her glasses.

"I brought your dinner," Grace said softly. "I didn't mean to disturb you."

"Uh, no. It's okay." Madison stepped back from the door to let her in and then shut it behind her. "I didn't mean to fall asleep. What time is it?"

"It's a little after six. You're not too late to join us for wine and hors d'oeuvres out on the back veranda, if you'd like. Or were you planning to go to the reunion cocktail party?"

"How did you know about that?"

"Oh, some of the other guests were talking about going." Grace set the tray on the table in front of the windows. "We have three gentlemen staying with us who are from your class. Two of them roomed together in school, so we put them in the two suites on this floor that share a bathroom. The other one is one floor up, in the Wisteria Loft Suite. Would you like to be introduced to them? Or maybe you already know them."

Madison gave her a taut smile. "No, that's all right."

"Okay, but you could still go to the party. I'm sure your friends are eager to see you."

"I don't know." Madison smoothed down her hair and grabbed her glasses from the nightstand. "I overslept, and by the time I eat and get ready—"

"I don't think it would hurt anything if you got to the party fashionably late," Grace said, setting out covered dishes and fresh coffee along with the napkin and silverware. "With events like that, people come and go all evening."

"I know, but tomorrow's picnic will be soon enough to see everybody. I don't think I'm ready for it tonight."

Grace pulled out a chair for her at the table. "It can be a little intimidating to spend time with people you haven't seen in a while, can't it?"

Madison sat down. "You could say that."

"Having something to eat will make you feel a little better." Grace took the metal cover from the plate. "This is chicken salad with avocado, mushrooms, and walnuts on homemade honey oat bread."

Madison looked faintly surprised. "That sounds good. Thank you."

"It's one of my sister's best recipes, and I hope you like the garlic oven fries too. They're not at all greasy, but they are very delicious."

"Thank you. And thank her too, if you would."

"I will." Grace took the cover off the smaller plate. "And I brought up a couple of our Italian almond cookies. We have some all-natural applesauce if you'd prefer, but I've found that these go better with coffee. What do you think?"

One corner of Madison's mouth turned up. "I think I need those cookies."

"All right then. Is there anything else I can bring you?"

"That's all," Madison assured her. "And, really, thank you so much."

"You're welcome." Grace hesitated, then said, "I know it can be difficult seeing your college friends after so many years, but I bet most of them are as nervous as you are."

Madison stared down at her plate but clearly wasn't seeing it. "I guess."

Again, Grace started to leave, and again something stopped her. Madison seemed so alone and so in need of a friend. "Madison?"

Madison glanced up, her dark eyes wide and uncertain. She reminded Grace of a doe on the edge of a clearing. "Yes?"

"I'm a pretty good listener. If you ever want to talk, I'm here."

"Oh, um, all right. Thank you." Madison fumbled with the little plate, almost dumping off the cookies in the process. "Should I bring the dishes down when I'm through?"

"No, no. You can leave them on the table. We'll get them when we clean your room tomorrow. Or, if you'd prefer, you can put them outside your door."

"Okay. Thanks." Madison gasped and scrambled to her feet. "I'm sorry. I forgot." She grabbed her purse from the dresser and started rummaging in it.

"No, no, no." Grace patted Madison's hand, keeping her from taking anything out of her purse. "A tip won't be necessary. I only wanted to make sure you're all right."

"I—" Madison began, and misery filled the brown depths of her eyes, then vanished behind a facade of polite calm. "I'm just tired. Thank you."

Grace nodded and tucked the empty tray under her arm. Maybe she'd said too much. Maybe she'd been too pushy. *Lord, don't let me have scared her off. Show her that I want to help.*

"You have a good night's rest then. Would you like a wake-up call in the morning?"

"In the morning?" Madison asked.

"If you're going to the picnic, you'll probably want to be up in plenty of time to be ready for it."

"Right. Yes, if someone could let me know when it's ten o'clock, that would be great."

"Ten o'clock," Grace said. "I'll make a note of it."

With a warm good night, she let herself out and padded down the stairs to the kitchen. She didn't want to pry into Madison's personal life, but clearly there was something troubling her. What could she do to help?

She was surprised to find her sister sitting at the kitchen table with a plate of hors d'oeuvres. "Charlotte. I thought you'd be out on the back veranda by now."

"Nope." Charlotte popped an hors d'oeuvre into her mouth. "You took dinner up to Buttercup. Dogwood isn't coming down. The guys in Bluebell, Rosebud, and Wisteria all went to their reunion cocktail party. There's nobody but us." She pushed the plate toward Grace. "Have one."

Grace sat down and took her up on the offer. "Mm, delicious. What is it?"

"Smoked salmon crostini. For what it's worth." She took a bite and made a face. "It's just as well no one's here to eat them. They need more garlic."

"Never mind," Grace soothed. "We certainly won't let them go to waste."

She heard a low whine from the floor and looked down to see Winston gazing at her with eyes of profound love. She glanced over at Charlotte.

Charlotte scowled back at her. "Oh, go ahead."

"Only one," Grace promised, and then she turned to the dog and made her tone stern. "Only one."

Winston gave a happy little yip and stood on his hind legs to take the treat from her. Then he went over to Charlotte and nuzzled her hand.

Charlotte shook her head and then smiled as she stroked his furry head. "Big, spoiled baby. You don't mind too little garlic, do you?"

"So, tell me about Wisteria," Grace said when Winston had stretched himself out under the table. "Obviously he checked in while I was upstairs."

"He came in when the other two guys were heading out to the party, and when they realized they were all here for the reunion, they decided to go together. I haven't even taken his bags up yet."

"So, what's he like?"

Charlotte shrugged. "I didn't get a chance to do more than check him in. Very attractive, well-mannered guy. He didn't say what he does, but I'd say from his luggage and clothes that he does pretty well."

Grace lifted one eyebrow. "Flashy, like the guy in Rosebud?"

"Not at all," Charlotte said with a giggle. "Thank goodness. No, this one is more of an introvert, from what I can tell. Friendly enough, but not the center-of-attention sort."

"Like the guy in Bluebell?"

"No, not really." Charlotte considered for a minute. "I think Bluebell is more the sidekick type. You know, the good-natured guy who goes along with the flashy guy's mischief and ends up being the only one who gets in trouble. Wisteria seems more like the quiet, brainy type."

"I guess we won't see much of them anyway. Not if they're going to all the reunion events."

Charlotte helped herself to another crostino. "It's what they're here for, right?"

"Yeah." Grace sighed. "Poor Madison up in Buttercup. She doesn't seem like she wants to relive her college days. I wish there was something I could do for her. And for Sarah too. I can't imagine how hard it must be to be jilted at the altar."

"It's sad, I know. That man ought to be ashamed of himself, whoever he is. It's not right to treat someone that way."

"I guess he had his reasons, whether or not they were good ones," Grace said. "I'm more interested in what Sarah's going to do going forward. She's trying so hard to put a brave face on things, but I can tell she's hurting. If she doesn't allow herself to grieve, she'll never be able to move past this."

Charlotte reached across the table and gave her hand a warm squeeze. "You can't solve everybody's problems."

"I want them to know somebody cares about them, but I guess I went about it all wrong. I don't think I helped either of them."

"Why do you think that?"

"I don't know." Grace bit into another crostino, though even her sister's excellent cooking couldn't cheer her up. "At this point, I don't even know how I can help."

"What did you expect on the first day? Give them a little time."

"I know. I didn't actually expect to solve anything, but I did hope to get them to let their guard down. Sometimes people just need someone to talk to."

"That's only if they feel like talking." Charlotte got up and went to the coffeepot. "Neither of them has been here for two minutes yet. Give them a little time to settle in. In the meantime, how about a cup of decaf? And we can figure out what to do for breakfast in the morning."

Grace nodded. Coffee would be nice. She had told Sarah things would feel better in the morning. She ought to take her own advice.

5

Sarah

The next morning, Sarah stared into the mirror above one of the his-and-hers sinks in the Dogwood Suite's luxurious bathroom. Was this basin his or hers?

"They're both mine," she muttered to the girl who stared back at her, the one with the frazzled hair, swollen eyes, and red, splotchy face. "The bed is all mine, the suite is all mine, and this honeymoon is all mine. All. Mine."

She blinked hard, refusing to let the tears well up again. If she stopped them now, by the time she bathed and dressed only half the people she came across today would know she had cried all night. That was a pretty good percentage, wasn't it?

In the spa tub, she treated herself to the decadently expensive bath crystals and body wash she had bought for her honeymoon. She followed that by a liberal application of a lotion that was supposed to give her skin "the soft radiance of a new day." What she wouldn't give for that to be true.

But once she had dried and styled her hair, then put on her new jeans and silk blouse in a shade of watermelon that added a nice glow to her face, she felt better. And she realized as she peered into the mirror that she looked better. A little tired, but no worse than that, especially with the touch of lipstick and mascara that gave her a casual-but-finished appearance. She picked up her big, floppy sun hat, thinking that after she ate she could go down to the lake and see what there was to do.

She was ready to face the day.

As ready as she would ever be.

She decided to have her breakfast on the inn's back veranda. It did have a wonderful view of the lake, and when Grace brought her coffee, freshly squeezed orange juice, and crab-and-shrimp quiche, she couldn't imagine anything better than being here alone to enjoy the food and the quiet. She was about halfway through when she heard the door open. The guy from yesterday in the lobby was heading toward her, his plate and coffee cup in hand.

"Hey, mind if I join you?" He moved her sun hat and sat in the wicker chair next to hers without waiting for her reply.

She shrugged and gazed out at the lake, but she couldn't help sneaking glances at him. He wore a black tank top under an unbuttoned green-on-green Hawaiian beach shirt and a pair of black cargo shorts. The sunglasses from yesterday were still parked on top of his head.

"I'm Keith," he reminded her. "Keith Chastain."

"Right."

She gave him a polite smile before returning to her coffee. It was great coffee, rich and aromatic. It wasn't flavored or a special blend. It was just plain coffee. Coffee-you-could-depend-on coffee. Good coffee was reliable. Good coffee was—

". . . never did tell me." Keith was watching her expectantly.

She had completely tuned him out. "I'm sorry, what?"

"You never told me your name," he said with a grin.

"Oh."

She blinked at him, her first instinct to politely but firmly let him know she wasn't interested. Then she remembered what she had told herself when she decided to come to Magnolia Harbor after all. She was here to have fun, not sulk. She decided to smile.

"Sarah O'Donnell."

"Nice to actually meet you, Sarah. Are you sure you're not here for the reunion? You're the right age and everything."

She gave him a slightly dubious expression, but evidently he was sincere. She guessed he was in his early thirties, which would be about right for a ten-year college reunion. No reason to tell him she was thirty, not quite as old as the people in his class.

She smoothed a lock of light-brown hair behind one ear. "I'm here to relax and enjoy myself. It's a nice place."

"All on your own?" he asked.

"I like it this way. I don't have to make any plans or keep to a schedule. I can do whatever I feel like doing whenever I feel like doing it. What could be better?"

There was admiration in his eyes. She liked that. After being humiliated the way she had been, she liked it a lot.

"Does that mean you don't have any plans for today?"

"Not a one," she said, "but you do. Where's your friend?"

"Who? Mike?"

Sarah nodded.

Keith shrugged and nodded toward the second floor. "He'll be down. He's calling his wife and kids."

"I thought most guys brought their wives to this sort of thing."

"That was the plan," Keith said, "but the kids got sick or something, so the wife stayed home to take care of them. Mike almost didn't come himself, but I talked him into it. We always hung out at school. I couldn't let him run out on me now, right?"

"A good friend always helps a guy keep his priorities straight I guess."

There was a touch of mischief in Keith's grin. "That's what I always say. Anyway, he ought to be down in a couple of minutes. He took his breakfast upstairs so he could talk and eat, but then we're going to the class picnic."

"Fun," Sarah said, turning again to her breakfast.

"It would be," Keith told her, "if you'd come too."

She raised an eyebrow at him. "I told you, I'm not part of the reunion."

"And I told you that we're allowed to bring guests. You can be my guest. What do you say?"

"Thank you very much, but no. I wouldn't know anybody there, and besides, I'm not dressed for a picnic."

"Aww, come on," he said. "You look great. Jeans go anywhere, and you've got this perfect picnic hat. It's going to be fun. There are all kinds of events planned and a big lunch later on and everything. Please come. I want to make every guy there jealous."

That brought an unexpected warmth to her cheeks. "Really, Keith, it's very nice of you to ask, and I—"

"Sarah."

She froze where she was, recognizing too well the low voice from behind her. Then she favored Keith with a coy smile. "I would love to go to the picnic with you, Keith. Let me finish my coffee."

"Sarah," the voice from the doorway repeated.

Forcing her expression into calm and pleasant lines, she turned. Slowly. He could wait. "Aidan. I have to admit, you're the last person I expected to see here."

She forced her heart from her throat and ordered it, without effect, to stop beating so fast.

Aidan.

The last time she had seen him, right after he had called off their wedding, those dark eyes had been smoldering with anger. His lean face had been flushed, his dark hair raked into disarray, and his hands clenched into tight fists. Now he was pale, his hair was slicked back, showing only a hint of natural loose curl, and his hands were stuffed into the pockets of his jacket. Why did he still have to be so handsome?

"I need to talk to you." He glanced uncertainly at Keith. "Please,

Sarah. Give me a minute."

"I think we already said everything there is to say." She put on her hat, stood up, and picked up her purse. "Now, if you'll excuse me, I have a picnic to go to."

She took Keith's arm, and together they swept past Aidan, but she paused and faced him again.

"I do want to thank you, Aidan," she said, making her voice syrupy sweet. "For the lovely honeymoon."

Keith chuckled and gave Aidan a nod. "See ya 'round, buddy."

Sarah turned again toward the lobby and caught a startled breath.

"I'm sorry," said the lady she had nearly run over. "I should have let you know I was right behind you."

"No, it was my fault. Excuse me," Sarah replied.

"We haven't met yet," the lady said. "I'm Winnie Bennett. My nieces, Grace and Charlotte, run the inn, so I pop by every now and again to see what's happening."

She must have been in her sixties, but there was light in her eyes and in her smile that made her seem younger. Sarah glanced back again to see Aidan still standing in the doorway to the veranda, and she couldn't help wondering how much this woman had overheard. Somehow, she felt ashamed, like when her grandmother had caught her disposing of broccoli casserole by giving it to her eager old beagle waiting under the table.

"I'm Sarah O'Donnell. I checked in last night."

"Grace told me." Winnie smiled at Keith. "You must be Mr. Chastain."

"Call me Keith."

"Keith." Winnie nodded and then rummaged in the pocket of the white linen jacket she wore open over a purple top. "I can tell you're both headed out, so I won't keep you, but I have something for Sarah."

She held out a beautiful antique hatpin. The pin itself must have been about eight inches long, and on the end was an amazing rhinestone butterfly.

"It's very sharp," Winnie said as Sarah took it. "Be careful."

"It's gorgeous." Sarah lightly touched the butterfly. "But I don't understand. This is for me?"

The older lady's smile grew impossibly brighter. "It is."

"But this is far too expensive."

"It's only a reproduction, but I think it's pretty. Don't worry, there's no obligation. I just thought you might need it."

Sarah studied the hatpin again. Awkward. What was she going to do with something like that? "Thank you, but I don't know what I'd do with it. It's beautiful, but I don't usually wear anything I could use it on. I mean—"

"Oh, I don't know." Winnie took her hat from her and examined it. "It's perfect for a nice big straw hat like this one. You don't have to actually use it to keep your hat on. You can add it for a little bit of flair. Why don't we give it a try?"

Sarah darted a sideways glance at Keith, who was looking equal parts amused and annoyed by this delay. She didn't dare see what Aidan was doing or even if he was still there.

"Um, okay."

She gave the pin to Winnie. After a moment of artistic consideration, Winnie set the pin at a jaunty angle at the right side of the crown of the hat and handed it back to Sarah. It did look cute.

"Now," Winnie said, "you're exactly right." She nodded in satisfaction and then, with a little wave, she walked toward the kitchen. "You two have a good time."

"Yeah, thanks," Keith said, starting Sarah toward the door again. "Good to meet you."

"Thank you!" Sarah called as they hurried off. She made sure to avoid Aidan's gaze.

"Come on," Keith muttered under his breath, "before she has to tell you about her old Grandma Myrtle who got that pin from some guy named Horace back in 1905 or something."

She giggled loud enough for the sound to carry back to the door that led out to the veranda and then let Keith escort her outside.

6

Charlotte

Charlotte peeped out of the kitchen when she heard the front door open and close, but she saw only Winnie. "They didn't stay at the table long. I guess I'd better go clear up."

Winnie nodded at the man coming toward them. A man she didn't recognize.

"Can I help you?" Charlotte said, with only a touch of wariness in her smile. "We usually only serve breakfast for our residents, but if you'd like, I can give you a list of restaurants you might enjoy."

"I didn't mean to intrude," the man said. "I . . . know someone who's staying here, and I was hoping to have a word with her."

"Miss O'Donnell," Winnie said.

"Yes. Miss O'Donnell. I hope that's not a problem."

He looked as if he had problems enough as it was.

"No," Charlotte said, her expression softening. "I just didn't hear you come in. Usually I do."

"I came in the same time as someone else was going out," he explained.

Charlotte remembered the guy up in Wisteria finishing his breakfast and leaving a few minutes before. "And I suppose you must have seen Miss O'Donnell. I heard her leave a moment ago."

"Yes. I saw her."

Winnie gave the man's shoulder a soothing pat. "Come by this evening. The inn serves wine, cheese, and hors d'oeuvres every evening between six and seven. It could be that Sarah will be back by then."

The man glanced at Charlotte. "No, I really couldn't. That's for your guests, I'm sure."

"I don't think the girls will mind." Winnie gave Charlotte her "I've got something in the works" expression, and Charlotte nodded. She'd learned a long time ago not to argue with Winnie.

"You're more than welcome, Mr. . . . ?"

"I'm Aidan Nicholson. And, if you're sure you wouldn't mind, I'll come. I'll be happy to pay."

"No," Charlotte told him. "You visit us anytime. We'll be glad to have you."

"Thank you." For the first time, he smiled, even if it was only a little bit. "Thank you very much. And thank you, Mrs. Bennett."

"You call me Winnie. And make sure you come back tonight."

"I'll do that," he said as he opened the front door. "I'm over at The Tidewater on the other side of the lake. See you tonight."

Charlotte scowled as he shut the door behind him. "The Tidewater. I should have known that snake Dean Bradley would be stealing our business."

There was a sudden twinkle in Winnie's eye. "Good grief, honey, the poor man already paid for a suite here when he and Sarah made reservations for their honeymoon. If he wants one at The Tidewater, is that so bad? Besides, you're full up. Did you want to haul an old mattress out to the barn and charge him to sleep there?"

Charlotte frowned at her. "Of course not. I guess I'm a little surprised he found a room over there. With this reunion going on, I would have thought The Tidewater would be booked too."

"Maybe there was a cancellation." There was still that twinkle in Winnie's eye. "Maybe he was meant to be here right now."

"I don't know why," Charlotte said, still frowning. "Sarah said he was the one who made other plans. Why would he show up now?"

Winnie only shrugged. "From what I just saw, those other plans must not have turned out the way he wanted them to."

"And she's supposed to run back to him the minute he snaps his fingers?" Charlotte rolled her eyes. "He sounds exactly like Dean. He thought he could do whatever he wanted to me and that I would take it and be grateful because he's so cute. Well, Mr. Cute Bradley will be waiting a long time for that to happen. I know he doesn't think it's possible, but I've moved on very nicely, thank you. I only wish he could be there to see me with my date tonight."

Grace

"Your date is tonight?" Grace asked as she came out of the kitchen. "Already?"

"Already," Charlotte said.

"But you told us about it only yesterday."

"No time like the present, right?" Charlotte glanced over at Winnie, who seemed more than a little bit startled. "What?"

"Nothing, dear." Winnie leaned over and kissed her cheek. "I'm glad you're going. You have a wonderful time, and I want to hear all about it later." She kissed Grace's cheek too. "I'll see you soon."

"You're leaving?" Grace asked. "You just got here."

"I did what I came by for. Now I have to get home and fix lunch for your uncle Gus and Phoebe."

Grace put her hands on her hips in mock reproof. "I happen to know you don't cook for your cat."

Winnie grinned. "She seems to come around for a taste of whatever it is we're having, so I guess I'm cooking for her too. Anyway, my Busy Bees meeting is tomorrow night, and if I don't make some decisions today about which fabrics I want to use in my new quilt and get all the prep work done, I won't have anything to work on."

"What are you going to make now?" Grace loved hearing about her aunt's projects.

"Another appliqué quilt. This one is all flowers and vines and lots of embroidery. I love the pattern, and I can't wait to get started."

"That one you showed us a picture of last month?" Charlotte asked. "The one that would be perfect for my cottage?" She gave Winnie a sweet smile and batted her lashes for good measure.

Winnie chuckled. "That's the one. And, yes, I get the hint. We'll see."

"She could give it to you as a wedding present," Grace suggested. "For you and your mystery date. Of course, it'll take her a few weeks to get it made, so you might have to put off the wedding until them."

"Funny," Charlotte said. "Very funny. But this matchmaker is extremely successful. She told me that over thirty percent of the people she matches end up getting married."

"A better question to ask her is how many of them stay married," Grace said.

"I'm not getting married anytime soon, okay? Even if this turns out to be the right guy. I learned enough by being around Dean Bradley to know I should take my time and keep my eyes open. Now I have dishes to clear away."

With that, Charlotte went out to the veranda.

"I don't know," Winnie said, watching her until she was out of sight. "She seems a little too determined to find someone right this minute."

Grace sighed. "She has been waiting a long time for the perfect guy. I'm glad she hasn't given up though. After what happened with Dean when they were working at *Le Crabe Fou*, I wouldn't blame her for being soured on men entirely."

"She never told me much about it," Winnie said. "Was it that bad?"

"Bad enough. And him opening The Tidewater right across the lake was the cherry on the pie in her face. I hope this new guy treats her better. More than that, I hope he's not in the restaurant or hotel business. I don't think she and Dean would have clashed nearly as much if they hadn't both been trying to make it in the same industry."

"They can't *all* be in the business."

Before Grace could reply, Charlotte came back toward the kitchen with an armload of dirty dishes. "Let me put these in the sink, and then we'd better do the rooms. Everybody's out, aren't they?"

"All at the reunion picnic," Grace said, "but before we go up, I need you to come to my room. I have something for you."

Charlotte's eyebrows went up. "For me?"

Grace nodded, unable to hide her excitement. "For tonight. Put the dishes in the sink and come on."

"Me too?" Winnie asked.

"Of course, you too." Grace squeezed her aunt's hand. "I want to know what you think."

After a brief rattle of dishes and silverware, Charlotte hurried back into the lobby. "Here I am."

The three of them went down the short hallway off the kitchen that led to Grace's private quarters. It wasn't a large space—only a bedroom, a bathroom, and a small living room nook—but it was done up in soothing neutrals and bathed in natural light from the tall windows and the French doors that led out onto the veranda.

When Grace shut the door after them, Winston popped his head up from where he had been sleeping on the overstuffed chair-and-a-half next to the bed. Seeing nothing of interest, he returned to his nap.

"This was going to be a gift for your birthday, but I think you might want it for your date tonight," Grace told Charlotte as she pulled open a drawer in her dresser and took out a rectangular cardboard box.

"Surprises are the best," Winnie said, looking on eagerly.

"My birthday's not for a couple of months," Charlotte said.

"I know." Grace put the box into her hands. "But I was afraid this would be gone if I waited to get it. And I know how much you liked it when we saw it at the store, so I thought I'd buy it and keep it for a special occasion." She smiled into her sister's eyes. "I think this is a pretty special occasion."

Charlotte looked a little flustered. "It's only a blind date. Not a big deal."

"It is a big deal. I'm proud of you for having the courage to do this, and for not letting your experiences with Dean keep you from trying again."

Charlotte set the box on the bed and wriggled off the lid. She gave a soft gasp.

"What?" Winnie tried to peek over her shoulder. "What?"

"Is this . . . ?" Charlotte pushed aside the tissue paper and lifted out what had been concealed under it. "It is! Oh, Grace, thank you."

She held the blouse against her, the shimmering peacock-green silk a perfect complement to her fair hair and dark eyes. Its understated elegance was ideal for a first date.

"I don't know what you had planned to wear, but I thought you might like this as an option."

"I was thinking my black tank with the floral overshirt," Charlotte said, running an admiring hand along the sleeve of the new blouse. "The guy might be a jerk after all."

"Or he might be Mr. Right." Winnie held the blouse up a little higher against Charlotte's shoulders. "Better wear this one."

Charlotte gave her sister a hug. "Thank you so much. But it's too much. I remember what the price tag said."

"Nothing is too much for my sister," Grace assured her. "And I'm glad you're doing this. You deserve someone wonderful, and I hope this top gives you the confidence to keep searching for him."

The bell over the front door rang.

"Rats." Charlotte refolded the blouse, laid it in the box, and replaced the lid. "There's one of the guests, and I haven't done any of the rooms yet."

"Don't worry," Grace said. "Leave that here for now if you want. I'll go see who it is. You sneak up and do that room while I keep him or her down here for a few minutes."

Winnie was already peeping out toward the reception area. "It's Sarah, the one in Dogwood."

"Okay," Charlotte said, "you two keep her talking and I'll go up the back stairs and get her room done as quick as I can."

"The sky won't fall if you don't finish before she goes up," Grace reminded her.

"I know, but I would rather not spoil the illusion that it's all done with fairies and pixie dust."

She hurried out of the room. Grace and Winnie went out into the reception area. Sarah was perusing the schedule of local activities Grace kept at the front desk.

"If there's anything you'd like more information about, let me know," Grace said. "I'll find out for you."

"Thanks. I'm not exactly sure how I'll spend the rest of the week. I suppose there's a trail that circles the lake."

Winnie smiled. "Only if you're up to walking the 285 miles around it."

Sarah gulped. "I had no idea it was so big. I think I'll stay a little closer to the inn."

"We do have some nice trails nearby," Grace assured her. "I can show you whenever you feel like going."

"Thanks. One of the things we—I mean, *I* have really enjoyed doing is getting out in the open and taking a nice long walk. It's hard to stay down when it's so pretty out, don't you think? Not that I'm down or anything. I'm just saying."

"I think you'll like the area," Grace said. "There's plenty of Spanish moss and magnolia blossoms, and that view of the water never gets old. Who could ask for more?"

"It is beautiful." Sarah put down the schedule and pushed her purse strap a little higher on her shoulder. "I may have you show me your favorite trail in the morning. For now, I think I'll get cleaned up and then relax for a while."

Grace looked at Winnie, widening her eyes. Charlotte wouldn't be through cleaning Sarah's room yet.

"How was your picnic, Sarah?" Winnie asked, not missing a beat.

Sarah made a little bit of a face. "It was all right. Very nice, in fact, but Keith kept running into old friends. After about the fifteenth 'hey remember that time we' conversation, I felt like I was invisible."

"That's too bad," Grace said. "Did Keith go up to his room?" Charlotte wouldn't be happy about that.

"He and five or six other guys from the baseball team decided to go to a sports bar and catch the Rangers game." Sarah sighed. "At least he paid for my cab back here."

Winnie pursed her lips. "He could have at least invited you to go along."

"He did. But I knew if I was invisible at a picnic, I'd be nonexistent during a baseball game with a bunch of ex-jocks and beer. Besides, I wanted to relax for a while. You're still having your little get together this evening, right?"

"You mean the wine and cheese?" Grace asked. "We certainly are. Every night at six sharp."

"Good. I'll definitely be there. Judging from what I had for breakfast this morning, I can tell the hors d'oeuvres will be heavenly."

"My sister will be glad to hear it."

"She's a great cook. You guys should start serving dinner. I bet it would be fabulous."

Grace held up one hand, laughing. "Oh, no. We have our hands full as it is. But who knows? Maybe someday we'll branch out."

"In the meantime," Winnie said, "you don't want to miss the hors d'oeuvres. You're right about how good they are. I think your friend from this morning is planning to come back and try them too."

Sarah wrinkled her forehead. "My—?" The warmth in her expression turned to ice. "You mean Aidan? The guy who crashed breakfast this morning?"

"'Crashed' is a little harsh, isn't it?"

"He's not a guest here. And I certainly didn't invite him." Sarah glared at Winnie, then gave a clearly forced smile. "I don't care either way. I'm not the one who walked out, and I don't have anything to be ashamed of."

"Good. You come tonight and enjoy yourself."

"Yes," Grace said, relieved to see Charlotte give her a nod from the kitchen door. "We'd love to have you, Sarah."

"Yeah, I'll be there." There was a hard edge to Sarah's smile. "I'm sure not going to hide from anybody." She touched the hatpin and nodded at Winnie. "Thanks again for this. It makes me smile every time I see it."

With that she strode across the lobby and up the stairs.

"I hope you know what you're doing," Grace told her aunt.

Winnie managed an expression of shocked innocence. "Me?"

"Yes, you. Sarah's mad enough at her ex already, and you're trying to make sure he comes back here after you've armed her with a razor-sharp, eight-inch spike."

Winnie chuckled. "I doubt she'll use it to commit serious bodily harm. Besides, I felt like she ought to have it. It looked cute on her hat."

"Yes, it did, and it made her smile. It was sweet of you to give it to her."

"You know how I am. Sometimes I feel led to give a particular item to a particular person, something I know will come in handy later on. I couldn't very well keep that hatpin when it's meant to be hers, now could I?"

"Of course not." Grace gave her a mischievous grin. "Does that mean you're coming to see what happens tonight?"

"I don't think so. I've done what I needed to do." She glanced at her watch. "Goodness, I've stayed much longer than I meant to. I'd better go. I'll see you girls later."

Grace smiled as she watched her aunt bustle out the front door and turn toward home. If anyone knew what she was doing, it was Winnie.

Madison

"Allow me."

Startled, Madison glanced up at the man who was reaching to open the inn's front door for her. She had seen him from a distance at the picnic, talking to some of the other guys. They'd all had the quiet, serious faces that generally meant they did something in the technical field, this guy most of all. But now that she saw him up close, she couldn't help thinking that he probably had a job doing something more creative. Something in art, perhaps. Somebody a graphic artist like her might have a lot in common with.

"Thank you," she said as he stepped aside to let her go in. She smiled tentatively. "You were at the picnic."

"I was."

His voice was low and rich, like the melted chocolate in the depths of his eyes, deep and mellow like the voice of a blues singer. *No*, she told herself sternly. She wasn't even going to consider actually talking to him. She didn't deserve a nice guy like him.

"Anyway, thank you." She stopped at the hatbox near the registration desk.

"You're welcome," he said, and she heard him cross the floor and go up the stairs.

Great. Now he thought she was a snob. So much for starting over.

She looked around the lobby, but it was empty. She heard low voices and general food-preparation sounds from the kitchen, but that was all. What would it hurt to take a peek?

Before she could lose her nerve, she snatched the lid off the hatbox. She could hardly believe it, but it was there—a sheet of the note paper that the inn provided for each suite. It was folded in half, and on the outside was one word: *MADISON*.

Wait. She hadn't signed the note she had left here. How would anyone know to put her name on the response? No, that was silly. The lady who owned the inn, Grace, had told her about the hatbox. Grace and her aunt knew she was interested in it. Why wouldn't they guess she had left a note there? And why wouldn't one of them have answered? They both seemed like the kind of women who wanted to help everyone, no matter what the trouble was.

Madison studied that one word, stark black on stark white. She didn't think it was a woman's writing, but she couldn't be sure. It was printed in neat block letters. Anyone could have written it.

MADISON.

What could it possibly say inside? Did she dare open it? She had to. It was addressed to her. It belonged to her. Why should she be afraid to know what was inside?

The sudden clash of pots and pans and then low laughter from the kitchen made her jump. If she was going to read it, she'd better do it before someone came in and caught her rifling the hatbox. Or better yet . . .

She tucked the page into the pocket of her jacket and practically vaulted up the stairs to her room. Once there, she shut the door behind her and stood leaning on it, panting as if she had just robbed a bank and had the police on her tail. Why should she be so nervous? The note was probably only some generic "don't worry, be happy" advice one of the ladies from the inn left for her.

"Don't be silly," she told herself firmly. "Open it and see."

She pushed herself away from the door, tossed her purse onto the dresser, and sat in the armchair in the corner of the room. In one quick motion, she unfolded the paper.

Madison, we all mess up. That doesn't make someone who messes up a bad person. The difference between a bad person and a good person is what that person does after messing up. Guilt is a heavy load. Too heavy for anyone to carry for so many years. But before you can settle things with the one you've hurt, you've got to forgive yourself. Forgiveness will release you both.

That was all. Forgiveness. How could she forgive herself? How could she possibly forgive anyone who had been so cruel and selfish? Someone who had willfully made someone's already hard life exponentially harder?

"How do I do that?" she said with a sob, gripping the note so tightly that she almost pulled it in half. "How do I forgive myself if he won't forgive me? And how can he forgive me if I'm too much of a coward to ask?"

All that afternoon, she, Kathy, Emma, and Kim had wandered around at the picnic looking for old friends, pointing out those they recognized, whispering about who had aged well and who had gone to seed, squealing and hugging and laughing too loud. All that afternoon, Madison had felt her heart race every time she saw a black man among the alumni, half fearing and half hoping she would see Marvin there.

Not that she would have spoken to him. Not right then anyway. But if she had seen him, if she could have asked one of his friends what he had done since graduation and if he had ended up all right, she might have gotten up the courage to say hello to him. To talk to him. Maybe even to tell him how sorry she was.

But she had been too afraid to ask about him. How terrible it would have been to have someone tell him she wanted to see him. He probably hadn't come anyway. Why should he have? He hadn't ever had many friends. He hadn't been the type to party and join all the clubs. He had always kept his head down, done his work, and then disappeared. It occurred to her now that she didn't have a clue what he had done outside of school. It was possible he'd had friends in his neighborhood. In his church? Surely he had church friends. Wasn't that where all the kids who didn't have a social life got together?

Anyway, she hadn't seen him. She had seen the guy who had held the door for her a minute ago. She had seen a number of guys who had played football and basketball, several who had been in theater and in music, a couple she remembered from the debate team, but no Marvin. He probably hadn't come. She didn't know if she was disappointed or relieved. She read the note again.

Forgiveness will release you both.

She needed to talk to him.

9

Sarah

The veranda was empty. Sarah checked her watch, the sleek little gold rectangle her parents had given her as a wedding present and insisted she keep. It was a couple of minutes past six. She should have waited longer to come down from her room. Now Aidan was sure to think she was waiting to see him. Okay, so she was, but only to let him see she was doing brilliantly without him. But, yeah, this would look bad. Too needy. She'd go upstairs again and give it another five minutes before she came back.

"You're not leaving, are you?" Grace came into the room, carrying a tray of assorted cheeses and some kind of fancy hors d'oeuvres. The wine was already on the sideboard. "I'm sure more people will be arriving soon."

Sarah smiled tentatively and sat down. "It's always a little awkward being the first."

"I'm sorry." Grace put the tray on the table and began setting out the food. "My sister and I try to make sure at least one of us is here early, but she's getting ready to go out for the evening, and these hors d'oeuvres needed a minute or two in the oven more than the recipe suggested."

"They smell delicious. What are they?"

"There are two kinds. Five-cheese gougères and ham-and-white-cheddar croquettes. Help yourself. I'd love to know what you think."

Sarah chose one of the croquettes, took a bite, and then closed her eyes as she gave a little sigh. "Oh, wow. That's divine."

"Thank you. They're one of my favorites too."

"Hey, Sarah."

Sarah turned to see Keith grinning at her from the doorway. "Keith. How was the game?"

"It was greatness. Me and Bobby and Dave had a little wager going on." He took a glass of wine and sat down next to her. "I was the one who came back with the cash."

She half expected him to pull the money out of his wallet and show it around. "That's good. As long as you had fun. What did you do with Mike?"

"Aw, you know. Mike got married and boring. He won't bet or drink or anything."

"I like remembering the parties I go to," Mike said coming over to sit across from them at the long table, a hint of amusement on his affable round face. "Not like when we were in school."

Keith rolled his eyes.

Mike smiled at Sarah. "I gave up being a frat boy years ago, I'm afraid. And I can't say I miss it." He showed her a photo of him with his wife and two young boys. "This is much better."

Sarah smiled at the picture, forbidding her tears to well up. She had always wanted to be the woman in that picture, the one with a couple of cute kids and a husband who was batty about her, even if he was balding and a little paunchy. She made her voice brisk and bright. "They're cute."

"Thanks." Mike gave Grace puppy dog eyes. "You have any more of those hush puppy things?"

Grace served him a couple of the croquettes. "Would you like to try the gougères too?"

"Sure. They sound great."

"Mike doesn't pass up a chance to try anything edible," Keith gibed.

Sarah was about to scowl at him, but then she noticed there was someone standing in the doorway to the veranda. Her heart raced. It was Aidan. Instead of scowling, she leaned toward Keith and laughed, making the laugh as light and flirtatious as she could.

"Hello," Grace said, noticing Aidan. "Please join us. We have two more guests coming, I believe."

"Thank you." Aidan came a step or two from the door. "Uh, Sarah, I was wondering if you'd talk to me for a minute."

"Sure," she told him. "It's a party. I usually talk to everybody at a party."

"Come on, Sarah. I'd appreciate it if you could give me a word or two. Privately."

"A word or two?" *How about two? "Get lost."*

"The music room isn't being used right now," Grace offered. "If you'd like a quiet place to talk, you're welcome to go there. It's at the front of the house."

"Sarah?" Aidan asked, his dark eyes pleading.

Keith narrowed his eyes at the newcomer. "You don't have to if you don't want to, Sarah."

"I know." Sarah gave him a little pat on the hand. "You'll wait for me, won't you? I'll be right back."

"I'll be here."

She and Aidan walked to the front of the house, neither of them saying anything until they reached a large, tastefully decorated space dominated by a black-lacquered grand piano.

"I guess this is the music room," Aidan said, peering inside, and then he stepped back a little, gesturing for her to go first.

She strode through the elegant room and sat in one of the two Louis XV chairs in the corner near the fireplace. Aidan took the other.

"Who's the guy?"

She gave him a cool glance. "Who wants to know?"

"Sarah." He exhaled and ran one hand through his thick hair. "I didn't come here to stir things up."

"Then why did you come here? To make sure I was miserable? Sorry to have disappointed you."

"Come on. I never wanted you to be miserable. I never wanted to hurt you."

She shrugged. "Could have fooled me."

He bit his lip and stared up at the elaborate chandelier that hung from the center of the ceiling. "I'm sorry," he said finally. "I know I've hurt you, and I know I've disappointed you, and I'm sorry."

He turned those contrite and wistful eyes on her, and she felt a little lurch in her heart.

She forced a tight smile. "Anything else you wanted to say?"

"I thought you might have cooled off enough by now to actually discuss the matter. I guess I was wrong."

"I guess you were." Her mouth tightened. "How am I supposed to feel? You dumped me right before we were going to get married. Right in front of all my friends and family. Practically at the altar. And you think I want to talk about it?"

"That's not exactly true," he said, his voice low and taut. "And it's not exactly fair. For one thing, I didn't dump you. You're the one who said we might as well call it off."

"And you're the one who did it!" Her face was already turning red. She could feel it. "I've never been so humiliated in my whole life."

"Sarah—"

She crossed her arms over her chest and lifted her chin. "Well?"

"I'm sorry," he said again. "I really am. Hurting you was the last thing I ever wanted."

"It didn't seem to bother you so much at the time."

"I got mad, okay? I never said I wanted to call things off, simply that we should consider slowing it down a little bit. We only met six months ago."

"Six and a half," she corrected.

"Six and a half then. And, yeah, maybe I shouldn't have asked you to marry me so soon, but I didn't think you'd go from getting engaged to booking the church in only two weeks."

"I told you that's what I was doing. You never said anything."

His eyebrows went up. "I didn't?"

"Okay, you might have said something about not having time to work everything out, but when I told you I'd take care of everything, you said okay."

"You were so excited about everything, I didn't want to spoil it for you."

She huffed. "So, waiting until everything was planned and paid for was a better time to spoil it than before anything had been done?"

"No, that's not what I mean. I just—"

"You *just* didn't actually love me enough to go through with it."

He shook his head. "That's not it at all. I told you I loved you. I told you I wanted us to get married. All I asked for was a little more time. But you wouldn't even let me explain. Every time I tried to talk to you, you hung up on me. You ignored my texts and my emails. I guess you threw my letters away. Did you even read them?"

She shrugged. "Why should I torture myself? It's over."

"Do you want it to be?"

His voice was low and alluring, tantalizing, mesmerizing, the way it had been when he had told her he wanted her for his wife.

Her throat tightened. "That's not the real question, is it?"

"What is, then?"

"The real question is if you're not sure now whether or not you want us to get married, are you ever going to be? I'm thirty, Aidan." Her voice cracked and she forced it to be steadier. "Thirty. How many more weeks or months or years am I supposed to wait around until you feel like you're ready to make a commitment?"

"That's never what I meant," he said, "but you wouldn't even listen."

She glared at him, her arms still crossed. "Well?"

"You're not making this very easy for me."

She didn't budge. She didn't want this to be easy for him. Not in the least.

"Sarah—"

"Hey, are you two done or what?" Keith looked into the room. "I figured since the door wasn't all the way closed, you must be through talking, right?"

"No," Aidan told him.

"Yes," Sarah said in the same instant.

"Sarah, you still don't understand," Aidan pleaded.

"I understand that things are over between us." Sarah gave him a cool nod and stood up. "So, if you'll excuse me, I believe I'd like some dinner." She smiled at Keith. "I sure hope you came here to suggest we go out somewhere."

"That's exactly it. What do you say? I hear there's a great Southern home-cooking place out on the highway."

"Oooh, yes, Aunt Patsy's Porch. Some of your friends from the picnic were talking about that place. I'd love to try it."

"Patsy's it is." He offered his arm, and she took it. "Good night, man. Better luck next time, right?"

Aidan didn't respond until she and Keith were at the door again. "Don't do anything stupid, Sarah."

Had he really called her stupid? She slammed the door behind her.

10

Charlotte

"I think I'm ready."

Charlotte turned her head so she could see her gold-and-emerald earrings—gold that enhanced the gold in her elegant chignon, and emeralds that picked up the peacock-green of the silk in her new blouse. She frowned thoughtfully at the pendant and bracelet that matched the earrings.

"Too much?" she asked her reflection for the second time, and for the second time she decided they were subdued enough to not be overwhelming. She didn't want to be overwhelming. Nothing was more pathetic than someone who was trying too hard.

She walked from her shabby-chic bedroom-living room and into her compact kitchen to get her car keys. She loved her cozy little cottage. Almost two hundred years old, the former chapel was snug and sturdy. Situated on the inn's grounds, it was a convenient walk away from work, yet far enough to be her own little retreat, big enough to suit her needs without being too much to take care of. In a word—perfect.

Tonight especially, she was glad she lived out here and not in the inn itself. It would be easy to slip inside tonight after her date and not have to answer a lot of questions about how it went. No matter how it went. She checked her appearance one final time in the small mirror by the door. She was ready.

Turner's Lakeside Grill was one of the most upscale restaurants in Magnolia Harbor. Charlotte had suggested the place to the matchmaker.

It was nice but not horribly expensive, and if the date turned out to be awful, she would be able to get home quickly. Still, the matchmaker had been in the business a long time. Charlotte didn't quite expect to meet the love of her life tonight, but she anticipated having a pleasant meal with a nice guy with maybe the hope that they would grow to be friends. That wasn't too much to ask, was it?

She was not going to think about all the horror stories she had heard from friends of hers who had been set up on blind dates. This had been arranged by a professional.

As usual, the restaurant was quiet on a Wednesday night, and no one was waiting to be seated. In the background, an easy-listening version of an old Beatles song played.

"Welcome to Turner's." The slim, blonde hostess smiled behind a sleek podium of polished cherrywood. "Table for one?"

"I'm meeting someone," Charlotte told her. "I'm supposed to ask for table twenty-seven."

"Right this way."

The girl led her past several minimalist cherrywood tables with gold accents and around a low wall of glass bricks with strings of opaque crystal disks hung above them. "The reservation specified a booth. I hope that's all right."

"Perfect," Charlotte said.

Only a few of the booths were occupied—two with couples, one with what looked like parents and their adult children. Only one, the one in the far corner, had a single occupant, his back to the wall.

Butterflies fluttered up from Charlotte's stomach and into her throat.

The man was studying the menu, so she could only see his dark hair, the sleeve of his black dinner jacket, and his well-groomed hands. Strong hands with the slender fingers of an artist or a craftsman. She was intrigued.

The hostess indicated the seat opposite him. "Here you are."

Hearing her, the man put down the menu and raised his head with an engaging smile. Then his brown eyes widened and the smile faded. "Charlotte?"

Charlotte blinked at him, frozen in place with her hand on the back of the booth and her ridiculous smile faltering. It couldn't be. It just couldn't be.

The hostess glanced from her to him and then back again. "Um, your waiter will be right with you."

With that, she disappeared, no doubt hurrying off to warn their waiter that there was likely to be drama at table twenty-seven.

"Dean," Charlotte whispered finally.

He gulped. "Uh . . . hi?"

"Dean Bradley, how dare you?" She put her hands on her hips, the blood boiling through her veins. "How *dare* you pull a trick like this? If you think for one minute I'm going to stay here and be humiliated, you've got another thing coming." She fished in her purse for her car keys. "And I'll have a word or two to say to that so-called matchmaker. I specifically said I didn't want to go out with any jerks, and if this isn't a breach of contract, much less proof of incompetence or even malfeasance, I don't know what is."

Her keys finally in hand, she turned to stalk out of the restaurant. Then she pulled up short. What was she doing? He wasn't getting off that easily. Not this time.

She stuffed her keys back into her bag and slid into the seat across from him. "On second thought, I'm not going. Not yet. First, I want you to know that I'm well aware of every sneaky, underhanded trick you've pulled on me since you worked for me at *Le Crabe Fou*. I know you stole my original recipes, I know you opened The Tidewater only to spite me, and I know you're trying to ruin things for me with

Chow Bella. But if you think a publisher like that would give you so much as a second glance, you're kidding yourself."

"Wait a minute—"

"You're the last man on this entire planet I would ever consider dating. You're arrogant, conniving, manipulative, selfish, heartless, and—and—"

He had been sitting there with his lips pressed into a thin line, his face a cold, impenetrable mask. Now he merely raised one eyebrow. "And?"

"Oooh, you see? That is exactly what I mean. You're so smug about everything." She stood again and snatched up her purse. "I am so done."

She made it halfway across the room when the heel on her left shoe broke. Somehow, she managed to catch herself against a wood pillar. With as much dignity as she could muster, she stepped out of both shoes, picked them up, and walked away.

She didn't look back.

11

Madison

Y*ou've got to forgive yourself.* Madison didn't know how many times she'd read those words since she had first opened the note from the hatbox. It was impossible. She had to make her pen pal understand.

Whoever you are, you don't have a clue what I've done or how much hurt I've caused. No, I haven't murdered anybody or anything like that, but I did destroy a life. I destroyed someone's dreams, someone's opportunity, and someone's hope. How do I forgive myself for that? More than that, how do I dare ask him to forgive me? Why should I be forgiven? How can I possibly think an "I'm sorry" will make up for the suffering I caused? There's no way I can give him back all the years I took from him, or the future I stole. How can I ever make it right?

She didn't read over what she had written. For all she knew, she had done nothing but ramble. But there it was. She needed to ask Marvin to forgive her, but she couldn't make herself do it. She'd never put this behind her if she didn't, but if she was honest with herself, she didn't want to. She didn't deserve to be free. Her own pain was nothing compared with what she had caused him. But she was so tired of carrying this around with her. Fifteen years. Wasn't that long enough?

You've got to forgive yourself.

"What do you know?" she muttered to the empty air. "Am I supposed to face myself in the mirror and say it wasn't a big deal? Marvin probably got over it, and he wasn't going to have that great a life anyway?"

She could still picture him, all arms and legs and glasses, crooked teeth, old-man pants that were too short, a voice that sometimes squeaked the few times he spoke up in class, and eyes—eyes that were too big for his skinny face, brown eyes full of humiliation and hurt. She had always avoided looking at his eyes and hurried off as fast as she could. And she was supposed to forgive herself for that?

Whoever had written the note was only trying to be helpful. At least this was an opportunity to get all of it off her chest. She'd kept everything bottled up for so long, she'd been afraid she was going to explode. "Don't expect someone else to fix your problems," her mother had always said, "especially the ones you made for yourself." So maybe she shouldn't expect her mysterious pen pal to actually tell her what to do. Maybe merely saying what was weighing on her mind would be enough. Maybe if she laid it all out so even she could figure out exactly what she was feeling, she'd have the courage to do something about it. Right now, it took every bit of resolve she had to take what she had written down to the lobby and put it into the hatbox.

"Please, God," she whispered as she slipped out of her room and down the stairs, "don't let anybody see me."

She crept toward the front desk, glancing around to make sure nobody was there. The lobby was empty. There wasn't a sound from the kitchen. Just as she put one hand on the hatbox, there was a rustle from behind the desk. She froze. What was she going to do? What would she say?

She snatched her hand away from the box and forced her expression into vague calm, waiting for whoever it was to stand up and ask her what she was doing there. Then she smiled.

"Hello there." She dropped to one knee as the dog, Winston, came toward her, his tail wagging and his eyes bright. "How are you, sweetie?"

She picked him up and cuddled him close. There was always something so soothing about holding a sweet-tempered dog or a cat. She could almost feel the tension seep out of her. He wriggled against her, licking her face as she walked to the hatbox and quickly slipped her note inside. Then she carried him over to the stairway and sat on the bottom step with him.

"Thanks for coming to see me," she whispered into his furry ear a few minutes later, and then she set him down and went back to her room. He followed her all the way, clearly eager to come inside.

"I'm sorry, boy," she told him, kneeling down again as she spoke. "I don't know if I'm allowed to let you into my room, and I don't want to bother anybody by asking right now. But I promise we'll have some time to play later on. How would that be?"

He tilted his head to one side, his button eyes still shining.

She hugged him again and then stood up. "Go on down now," she said, gesturing to the stairs. "I'll see you later."

He let out a little breath and then trotted slowly away. At least the dog liked her. She felt better already.

Madison slept well that night—much better than on her first night at the inn. Well, to be honest, it was her first good night's sleep since she had forced herself to make plans to be at the reunion. Simply admitting her fears must have been good for her. Still, she couldn't help being curious about what her correspondent would say in reply to her last note. She got up a little earlier than usual, dressed for the softball game and lake party planned for later in the morning, and then made her way down the stairs.

A quick glance around told her she was alone, but there was no predicting when one of the other guests might come downstairs or whether someone from the obviously busy kitchen would pop her head out to see who was at the front desk. A little shiver of anticipation tingled down her spine as she lifted the hatbox lid.

There was nothing there. Nothing but the notes that had already been in the box when she had arrived on Tuesday. Even her pen pal had abandoned her.

Or had he? Her note from last night was gone. Perhaps he had picked it up this morning. Or maybe he had gotten it last night and hadn't brought down his reply yet. She wondered who it could be anyway. Of course, she couldn't be sure it was a man. The handwriting was a little ambiguous. The owner of the inn, Grace, was definitely the type to counsel her to forgive herself. It could also be Grace's aunt, Winnie.

If it was a man, there weren't that many options. That Keith guy? Hardly. He was too full of himself to do more than drink, brag, and chase after the woman in the Dogwood Suite. Then there was the guy up in the loft. He seemed nice enough, very polite and everything, but not the kind of guy who would answer anonymous notes from a hatbox. He was all business. The guy in the Bluebell Suite, Keith's friend Mike, might be the one though. He might be only her age, but he was a dad. Dads tended to be fixers, right? Plus, he seemed to care about people. And, from what she had seen, he never let Keith's gibes get to him. But was he the sort of guy who—

"I'll go see."

Madison started at the voice from the kitchen. Grace? Her sister,

Charlotte? Not wanting to be caught with her hand in the cookie jar, Madison bolted toward the door that led out to the veranda.

Grace reached the front desk before she noticed Madison. "Oh, good morning. You're down early."

Madison was near enough to the door by then for it to look as if she had come down the stairs and headed straight to the veranda—she hoped. "Good morning. I hope not too early." She smiled as if the only thing on her mind was breakfast. "Should I come back down later?"

"Not at all." Grace smiled and came toward her. "The food's not quite ready yet, but I'll be happy to bring you some coffee. It's freshly brewed. Or we have orange juice if you'd prefer."

"Some coffee would be great, but no hurry. I'm going to go sit outside and enjoy the view."

"It's a great way to start a morning, isn't it?" Grace said. "No matter what I have on my mind, it seems to help me remember how much is right in my life."

Madison nodded and went out to the veranda. Now why had Grace said that to her in particular? Was she the one who had replied to the notes after all?

Or Grace is just a nice lady who would have said that to anyone. She wasn't going to drive herself crazy over this. Not this morning anyway. She'd have a nice breakfast and then enjoy herself at the softball game. Maybe if she spent a little more time with Kathy, Emma, and Kim, she'd feel a little less awkward with them. They had been so close at school, but when she had finally gotten past the hugs and squeals and catching up at the picnic yesterday, she had begun to wonder why that was. If she had met them now, at thirty-two rather than fifteen, would they have anything in common?

The three of them were married. Emma and Kim were full-time mothers whose children had recently started school. Kathy was the

CEO of a communications company who supported her modern-artist husband. Madison was happy to see things had turned out well for all of them, but she really didn't know them anymore. All they seemed interested in was making snide remarks about the other people at the reunion and one-upping each other about their homes and their cars and their wardrobes. Madison had never felt so out of place in all her life.

"God," she whispered into the cool, quiet morning, "why am I even here?"

Apart from the chatter of a pair of wrens in the nearby magnolia tree, there was no answer.

A few minutes later, Grace brought her a steaming cup of coffee. "Your breakfast is nearly ready. I'll be back."

Alone again, Madison closed her eyes and breathed in the fragrance of roasted arabica beans. That's all she had to think about right now—this one moment of perfect peace.

"Hello."

Startled, she opened her eyes and saw Keith's friend, Mike, smiling down at her.

"I hope I didn't disturb you," he said, sitting across the table from her. "I wanted to get an early start so I can give my family a call before the softball game."

She sat up a little straighter. "You haven't disturbed me at all. It's nice you want to keep in touch."

He shrugged, his expression a little abashed. "I didn't want to come without my wife, but Angie said I ought to go ahead and have a good time. No use both of us staying home because the kids are sick."

"That was understanding of her. I hope it's nothing serious."

"Just a stomach bug," he said. "The doctor says it's not a big deal. But, come on, how can she expect me to have much fun without her?" He chuckled at himself. "I guess we're supposed to pretend we're still in college here, but I've got it too good right now to want to be twenty again."

She stared at him until he seemed sort of self-conscious.

"I never was one of the cool kids," he admitted, but then he grinned. "Amazing how little I care about that now."

She couldn't help smiling back. "I guess it takes a while to figure out who you are and what you truly want out of life."

"That's what college is for, I suppose. I regret wasting most of it trying to be like everybody else. I think I'd have impressed everybody a lot more if I hadn't tried so hard to impress them." He laughed a little. "If that even makes sense."

"Yeah." She wasn't smiling anymore. "It's hard to be that strong at that age. And when you look back and see how much you've messed up . . ."

Her throat tightened and she couldn't go on.

"I guess we all have that," he said. "You can't change the past. You can forgive yourself and go on."

Forgive yourself. Was it odd that he should say that? It wasn't as if that was a particularly original thought. But for him to happen to say it right now . . .

"Good morning," Grace said to Mike as she came in with a tray. "I thought I heard you come down, so I went ahead and brought you breakfast and some coffee."

She set down two plates of crepes filled with scrambled eggs, tomatoes, and cheese. There was fruit on the side and some sausage links that smelled like they had exactly the right amount of sage in them.

"Great," Mike said, unrolling his napkin and putting it in his lap. "Thanks."

"More coffee?" Grace asked Madison, taking the pot from the tray.

Madison nodded just as Keith stepped out onto the veranda with the girl from the Dogwood Suite. The guy from the loft was behind them. She should probably put some names with faces, but she didn't know if it really mattered. She wouldn't see any of them again.

Grace served everyone coffee and brought them breakfast, and soon the general conversation turned to the softball game. It seemed that Sarah, the girl in the Dogwood Suite, was going to come with Keith. The guy from the loft, Donny, said he wasn't much of an athlete, but that he was going to give it a shot. He was wearing a Texas Rangers shirt, open down the front with a black tee underneath. He was obviously ready to play.

"You're coming, right?" Mike asked Madison. "It ought to be fun."

"I haven't played much since I was in high school," she admitted. "I wasn't too bad back then, especially running bases, but that's been a while. Now I'm mostly into Pilates."

Donny gave her an enigmatic smile, which was even more intriguing on his handsome face. "I'm guessing you're a runner. What do you say?"

"I don't know. I'd probably have to change."

"You've got on tennis shoes and jeans," Sarah said, studying her thoughtfully. "Tuck in your top and you ought to be fine. Maybe put your hair in a ponytail or something."

Madison pulled her springy curls back and started rummaging in her purse with her free hand. "I have a hair tie in here somewhere, I think. Are you going to play?"

"Well, I—"

"Of course not," Keith said with a smirk. "Gotta have somebody in the stands watching me, right?"

Out of his line of sight, Mike rolled his eyes.

"I'm not much of an athlete," Sarah said.

Madison found a navy-colored elastic band in her purse and twisted it around her ponytail. It would go well enough with her black high tops, new jeans, and old red T-shirt. The shirt had the college logo on it, but it was so faded, she had almost decided against bringing it with her to the reunion. But it was perfect for the softball game and lake party.

"Looks good," Donny said with a little bit of a nod, and then he went back to his crepes.

Madison smoothed her hair once more. "I guess I'll give it a try."

"Good." Mike toasted her with his coffee cup. "It'll be fun."

The softball game was held only a stone's throw from the lake. It wasn't anything more than a freshly mowed field with sandbags set out for bases and a pitcher's mound. There was nothing formal about the game, though the people who had actually been on the teams in school tried to make it at least organized. The former captain of the men's team and the former captain of the women's team took turns picking players from the mixed group and ended up with two fairly evenly matched rosters.

Madison was picked for the same team as Keith, and Mike and Donny ended up with the opposition. After a few nervous moments, she was surprised to realize how much fun it was to play without any kind of deadline or pressure to perform. She got two strikes the first time she was at bat, but her third swing popped the ball into the outfield, barely over Donny's outstretched glove. He scooped it up and threw it, but not before two of her teammates scored and she was safe at third.

With a little bit of a smile, Donny shook his head and pointed at her. Obviously, he didn't intend to let that happen again. She made sure her own smile said "watch me."

After six innings the score was tied, and the people in charge of after-game snacks were already setting out food. The other team scored twice in the seventh, Mike stealing one from third, but at the bottom of the inning, Keith slugged a ball deep into the underbrush and then moonwalked around all the bases and home before it was found.

"Ham!" Mike called from center field, and Keith merely waved as if he were riding a parade float.

They had two outs and were still down one when Madison was up two batters later.

I don't have to win this, she told herself. *I only have to tie it and make sure it at least goes to extra innings. And not mess up.*

On the first pitch, she missed by a mile.

"Strike!" called the gangly red-haired girl who was playing umpire.

"Hang in there, baby!" Keith shouted.

Madison wiped her sweaty hands on her faded shirt and tightened her grip on the bat. On the next pitch, she blasted the ball into right field. With her teammates screaming, she dropped the bat and started to run. The right fielder scooped up the ball, panicked, and threw it way over the first baseman's head and into center field. Madison hit the base and kept running. By the time she reached second, Mike had caught the ball and tossed it toward third. Everyone was screaming as the girl playing third bobbled the ball.

"Get it! Get it!" Mike howled.

Quick as a cat, Donny grabbed the ball and sprinted after Madison down the baseline. She tagged third and headed for home with him right behind her.

"Slide!" everyone on her team screamed. "Slide!"

"Get her!" roared Donny's team.

Everything happened in a split second. He was gaining on her, she could feel it. She'd have to slide. *Ugh*, she was too old for this, but she did it anyway.

If she had imagined a graceful, balletic glide into home, she was sadly mistaken. Her right leg went forward, but her left leg didn't cooperate. She didn't know how she managed it, but she landed hard on her backside with Donny diving right beside her, all of it accompanied by the ominous sound of ripping denim.

The world seemed to stop.

Everyone on both teams looked at her and then the umpire.

"I couldn't see," the umpire told them. "So, what's the deal, Madison? Are you out or not?"

Madison's foot was on home base. Donny stood up and offered her his hand.

"I'm out!" Madison called, and the other team started whooping and slapping each other on the back. Everyone but Donny.

"I never touched you," he said, his voice low. "You scored."

She pressed her lips together, her eyes stinging with mortified tears. "I'm out," she murmured. "Please. I'm out."

He dropped to one knee beside her. "Are you hurt? What's wrong?"

"I can't get up," she hissed. "Please go away and let me die."

"It can't be that bad. Let me help you to one of the chairs over there and then we can get you to the ER or something."

"You don't understand. Please go."

"Everything okay?" Mike asked, loping up to them. Several other people were watching them with concern.

"Sure," Donny told him. "We'll be right there. You'd better hurry before all the cookies are gone."

With a chuckle, Mike headed to the snack tables with everyone else.

"Now tell me what's wrong," Donny asked, keeping his voice low. "Are you sure you're not hurt?"

She squeezed her eyes shut, wishing she could sink into the ground right there, but he seemed so worried that she had to tell him.

"I'm not hurt," she said. "I split the seam in my jeans."

There was a sudden twinkle in his dark eyes, but there was understanding and sympathy there too. Without a word, he took off his Rangers shirt.

"Put it on. It's pretty long, and it'll go with your outfit. Nobody will ever know anything happened."

He pulled her to her feet, standing behind her to shield her from prying eyes, and helped her into the shirt. As he had told her, it was long, reaching about halfway to her knees.

"Thanks." She glanced over at the crowd around the snack table. "I'll get this back to you right away."

"No rush. Ready to get a bite to eat?"

Her eyes widened. "I couldn't. I'd better go on back to the inn."

"It's not that bad, is it?" he asked.

"Yeah, it is."

"I have an idea. Tell everybody you're going to change and you'll be right back."

She frowned at him. "I am not telling everybody I split my pants."

"Of course not. Tell them you want to freshen up after the game." There was a touch of admiration in his eyes. "Girls like you never want to have a hair out of place. Nobody will think anything of it. It won't take more than a few minutes to get over to the inn and back."

"I don't know. It's too embarrassing."

"Not if you don't let folks know you're embarrassed." His mouth tightened almost imperceptibly. "Keep your head up, and don't let anybody know anything's wrong."

He nodded toward the rest of the group, and she took a deep breath. She could do this.

"Hey, what'd you give her your shirt for?" one of the guys on Donny's team asked as she and Donny approached the tables. "Lose a bet?"

Donny chuckled. "You always guess right, Jack. I wasn't sure she'd try that slide, but maybe she's braver than she thinks."

He gave her an encouraging smile. *Go on*, it said. *You can do this.*

"I'm definitely grubbier than I thought I would be." She smiled. "I'm going to run back to the inn and get cleaned up. I don't want to spend the rest of the afternoon smelling like you guys."

The girl who had been the umpire made a face while the guys hooted with laughter.

"Back in a bit," Madison said, and head held high, she walked out to her car. As she got behind the wheel, she was almost certain she saw Donny give her a subtle nod. He was such a nice guy. Too bad she didn't deserve somebody like him.

No one was behind the reception desk when Madison got back to the inn, so she risked a quick peek into the hatbox. There was another note with her name on it. Her heart rate surged as she snatched it up, slapped the lid onto the box, and dashed up the stairs to her suite.

It was addressed to her in the same writing as the one before. It hadn't been there before she went in to breakfast, so that most likely ruled out Donny as her anonymous pen pal. Even though she had thought him an unlikely choice, she was disappointed. The more she was around him, the more she had thought he might be the type to give her the sort of gentle advice the first note had offered.

She took off his baseball shirt and laid it over a ladder-back chair. Then she stripped off her ruined jeans and put on a pair of shorts. So much for high price being a guarantee of good quality. After that, she sat again in the overstuffed chair in the corner to read the note.

Madison,

If you were actually a bad person, if you were as "petty and thoughtless" as you think you are, then this wouldn't still be bothering you. It would never have bothered you in the first place. As long as you have a conscience that can be pricked, you have a heart that can make things right. If you were in school when this particular incident happened, you must have been very young. Young people don't always realize the consequences of their actions. They don't always realize how they hurt others. And often it isn't selfishness or even thoughtlessness but fear and insecurity that makes them act in hurtful ways. Part of growing up is fixing past mistakes as much as possible. Look back on that schoolgirl, at what was truly in her heart back then, and show her a little grace. Has she learned from what happened? Has she grown? Has she asked God to forgive her, even if she hasn't yet asked for forgiveness from the person she wronged? If so, can't you forgive her too?

Had she asked God?

Madison swallowed down the tightness in her throat. She shouldn't have read the stupid thing right now. She had to get cleaned up and back to the reunion. She certainly couldn't show up with red eyes and a blotchy face. She couldn't think of anything that the note said. It would spoil everything.

A quick look around told her the room had already been cleaned that morning, so she tucked the note under the plump pillow for later. It was time to go to the lake party before anyone started wondering if something was wrong.

12

Charlotte

Once she and Grace had washed and put away the breakfast dishes and then tidied all the rooms, Charlotte made her way to Hanson's Farm Fresh Foods on the west side of Magnolia Harbor. Cal Gunderson, whose maternal grandfather was the last actual Hanson to run the store, greeted her with his usual welcoming smile. With his pleasant, apple-cheeked face, all he needed was a handlebar mustache and a straw hat to give the impression that he had stepped right out of 1912 when the store had first opened.

"Charlotte. I was hoping you'd be in today. I put back some gorgeous asparagus for you, if you're interested."

"Always," she told him, admiring some mouthwatering white grapes displayed with the rest of the fruit. "It's not on my list, but when you say something's good, I know I ought to add it."

"I'll never steer you wrong," he said, and then he chuckled. "Not about fresh produce and dairy products anyway. But don't ask me about the stock market."

"Same here," she said as she checked her list for anything she might need his help with. "Do you happen to have any more of that blue cheese you had a couple of weeks ago? It made a great quiche, and I'd like to do it again for the guests we have now."

"Hmmm, I know I told the wife to keep some of that for you, but I don't recall seeing it in the dairy case. Let me go check in the back."

He disappeared through the door behind the checkout counter, and Charlotte helped herself to a shopping cart. She and Grace insisted on the very best fresh fruit and vegetables for their guests, and if that meant going shopping three or four times a week, so be it.

The first thing she put into the cart was a bag of those luscious grapes. They'd go well with the merlot, Taleggio cheese, and freshly baked Italian bread she had planned for this evening. Or perhaps she ought to get those plump strawberries next to them instead. Hanson's always had such delicious produce, it was hard to choose. Of course, she could serve them tomorrow night, or maybe they would be better in the next morning's crepes.

After a moment's hesitation, she put the strawberries in the cart alongside the grapes. It was hard to buy exactly the right amount of any one thing, hard to know if any particular item would be snatched up and devoured as soon as it was put out or would sit until it was too spoiled to eat. She didn't care. She liked strawberries and grapes. She'd eat them if no one else did.

She was about to move on to where Cal kept the fresh eggs when she heard someone call her. Recognizing the lilting Oxford accent, she turned and smiled at her pastor's wife.

"Hello, Penny. How are you? And how's Pastor Glen?"

"We're both very well, thank you." Petite and blonde, Penny Abrams was still fresh-faced and lively despite her nearly sixty years. "How are you?"

"I'm fine. I was only—"

"How are you really?" Penny put one hand on Charlotte's arm, her dark eyes filled with concern. "I promise you I didn't believe a word of it. Not a single word. And I said as much right then and there. And Angel backed me up."

Charlotte frowned, puzzled. "Angel at the coffee shop?"

Penny nodded.

"She backed you up about what?"

Penny clapped a hand over her mouth. "I'm sorry. I thought you knew. I was sure someone must have mentioned it to you already, and I wanted you to know that I made sure and told them the very notion was ridiculous."

Something cold and heavy congealed in the pit of Charlotte's stomach. "No, no one mentioned anything to me. What are you talking about?"

"Oh, dear. I'm so sorry. I hate gossip, and if I hadn't thought you needed some shoring up over it about now, I wouldn't have said a thing. I'm sure it will blow over."

Charlotte licked her lips. It must be something bad. "What did they say?"

"It was one of those 'someone heard from someone else' things." Penny winced. "You know how talk spreads. Anyway, somebody said that you didn't actually create the special sauce you use on your eggs Benedict, and that you—well, that you stole the recipe for that wonderful crab-and-shrimp quiche you serve at the inn. Those were the only two they mentioned, because I stopped them right there and said there couldn't be a word of truth to it. I said if you advertised them as original recipes, then that's what they are, and they shouldn't even listen to rumors like that, much less spread them."

Charlotte felt vaguely nauseous. "Who are 'they'?"

"I'd rather not say, but I'm sorry to have upset you. I thought surely you already knew."

"Then it's already all over town," Charlotte said bleakly.

"Dear Charlotte." Penny gave her an impulsive hug. "I don't know if it's as bad as that, and I tried to cut it off as best I could. Surely no one who knows you will believe it for an instant."

"I'm sure they wouldn't." Charlotte forced a smile. Perhaps nobody who knew her would believe it, but what about everyone else, especially potential guests? "Thanks for letting me know what was going on. And thanks for trying to stop it."

"I'm so sorry," Penny murmured again. "Do let us know if there's anything we can do to help."

"Found it!" A triumphant Cal brought over a slab of blue cheese. "Last of it, of course, but I can add more to my order with the wholesaler if you'd like."

Having forgotten their discussion earlier because of her conversation with Penny, Charlotte gaped at him for a second or two before her memory returned. "Uh, thank you, but I think this will do for right now. I might have you get more later on."

"Anything you say. Are you ready to check out, Mrs. Abrams?"

"Yes, thank you," Penny said, and she gave Charlotte's hand a quick pat. "Keep your head up, dear. We're with you."

She and Cal went to the register, chatting about the price of coffee beans, and Charlotte started toward the dairy section, hardly seeing what was on her list. How dare someone accuse her of stealing her own recipes? She had worked hard on all of them, the quiche especially, getting every ingredient, every bit of seasoning, and every nuance of the presentation exactly right. She was proud to add *Signature Dish* next to her special creations on the inn's menu. They were the product of her years of study, observation, and experimentation, and she had added a lot of her own creativity too. Her food was a form of self-expression.

She huffed as she picked up two gallons of fresh milk and some locally made honey butter. Whoever had started this rumor was not only damaging the reputation of the inn, they were impugning her character. It would take a pretty low-down snake to do that when there was absolutely no truth to it and no reason to even suspect it. And she was pretty sure she knew the name of the snake.

Grace came down the back stairs while Charlotte was putting away the groceries.

"Everything okay?"

Charlotte slammed the refrigerator door. "Sure. Why wouldn't it be?"

"You don't usually put the dishwashing detergent in the fridge and the tomatoes under the sink. And you never do it so . . . violently."

"Oh."

Charlotte put the tomatoes in the fridge and the detergent under the sink. Of course Grace would notice something was bothering her. She could always sense when anyone was troubled. Or angry. Or both. *Okay, mostly angry.*

Grace poured out two glasses of sweet tea from the pitcher in the refrigerator and sat down at the kitchen table. "Want to talk about it?"

Charlotte sat across from her. "I saw Penny Abrams at Hanson's."

"And?"

"She told me there's a rumor going around town that I stole my original recipes."

"What?" There was a flash of anger in Grace's eyes. "Why would anyone say something like that? It's ridiculous."

"I don't know why," Charlotte told her, "but I'm pretty sure who."

"Now, be fair, Charlotte. Unless Penny told you something that gives you a good reason to suspect—"

"No, don't argue with me. Who else would have any interest in ruining my reputation? Who else would benefit from giving the inn a black eye?" She leaned forward and jabbed a finger against the counter as she spat the name. "Dean Bradley would be delighted to see us go under. And, especially after our so-called date, the more he can humiliate me, the better."

"That's a little harsh, isn't it? From what you told me, he was as surprised as you were about the date. It's not like he planned for it to be you."

Charlotte scowled at her sister. Why did she always have to be so sensible?

She tried a different approach. "You know he stole my recipe for stuffed pork chops when he worked for me at *Le Crabe Fou*. 'Tidewater Pork Chops' my foot! How like him to accuse me of doing something he's actually guilty of."

"Are you sure about the pork chops?" Grace asked, and her tone was insufferably reasonable.

Charlotte snorted. "Please. Do you really think changing one or two ingredients is enough to make me not recognize my own creation?" She didn't wait for an answer. "But that's neither here nor there. I am going over to The Tidewater this minute to tell him I know what he's doing and that he'd better cut it out right now."

"Wouldn't it be best to let this all blow over? I don't suppose Penny told you who said something about the recipes in the first place."

"No. The poor thing thought I already knew about the rumors and was trying to be supportive. I could tell she felt so bad when she realized she was the first to tell me about it. She didn't want to stir up more trouble by mentioning any names, but she did tell whoever it was that there was no truth to it." Charlotte glared down into her untouched glass of tea and then took a soothing drink. "Anyway, if she overheard someone talking about it, that probably means it's been passed around more than once. Dean ought to have to make a public apology."

"Now, Charlotte—"

"He should have to write it out on that *très chic* menu board he has in the lobby of The Tidewater." Charlotte giggled. "In all capital letters at least six inches high. And I want him to post flyers in all the shops in town."

"Now you're being silly," Grace said, but she grinned too. "Laughing it off is the best thing you could do, especially since you don't have anything to go on but hearsay."

Unfortunately, she was right. Charlotte knew she had no proof against Dean, only her own unfounded assumption. She was about to change the subject when a new thought hit her, and she gasped.

"What if this gets back to my publisher? I have a moral turpitude clause. Chow Bella could terminate my contract like that." She snapped her fingers. "And that's exactly what Dean would love to have happen."

"But you haven't done anything wrong," Grace protested.

"It doesn't matter. If they think I've made them look bad, or if they're concerned that I might, they can terminate the contract. Even if I convince them I'm not guilty, they could decide not to sign me for any more cookbooks because the public thinks I'm a fraud."

"Whoa, whoa. That's going a little too far, isn't it? A couple of gossips in Magnolia Harbor, South Carolina, doesn't exactly add up to the public in general, do they?"

"News gets around." Charlotte bit her lip, not knowing if she felt more like screaming or crying. "Especially with everybody being on social media. Good heavens, it could be all over the world by tomorrow!"

"Calm down. You're not Martha Stewart or Paula Dean. As popular as your books have been, you're not exactly a celebrity yet." Grace's expression was full of understanding and sympathy. "Why don't you take a minute or two to drink your tea and then go call your editor? Tristan must have dealt with this sort of thing before. I'm sure he can tell you whether you ought to be worried about it at this point, and he'll probably have some idea of how to handle it."

Charlotte took a deep, calming breath. "You're right. Working in New York City, he has to have seen a lot worse than this." She took another deep drink. "All I have to do now is work up my courage."

"I'm sure he'd rather hear it from you than on the news. And I'm sure he'd appreciate knowing as soon as possible about anything that might become a problem later."

Charlotte sighed. "I guess." With sudden resolve, she tossed back the rest of the tea and then got to her feet. "Do you mind if I use your room? I'd like a little privacy, and I'd rather not walk back to the cottage."

"Help yourself." Grace stood, too, and gave her a tight hug. "And try not to worry. You haven't done anything wrong."

"I hope I can convince Tristan of that."

Charlotte headed toward Grace's room, trying to focus on the likelihood that this was only a tempest in a teapot and not the bleak prospect of suddenly being without a publisher.

Sarah

The Tidewater was sleek and modern, beautifully situated across the lake from the Magnolia Harbor Inn. As she sat eating breakfast on the veranda, Sarah could see it gleaming there across the water, all glass and stone and polished wood. She wondered idly if one of the upper windows was Aidan's, and then she stopped herself. She was not going to think of him. It was no use now that it was too late, and she wasn't such a doormat that she would go running back to him simply because he asked her to.

She took a bite of her cinnamon polenta pancakes, sweet and tart with their blueberry-cranberry topping, and gazed along the shore on her side of the lake. It looked as if it was going to be a warm day, and the sparkling water practically called to her. She could take a long swim by herself and relax. Keith had said something about wanting her to go with him and everyone else at the reunion to a drag race that afternoon, but she hadn't given him an answer yet. A lot of people enjoyed racing, but it wasn't that high on her personal list. Aidan would have taken her to see some local craftsman work or to a carnival with cheesy rides and rigged games or swimming in the lake. They'd had so many plans for this week.

"Hey!"

Sarah looked up to see Keith coming out onto the veranda.

"Good morning, Keith."

"You looked bored." He plopped himself down into the chair

next to hers. "No plans for this morning? You still haven't told me if you're coming to the race with me."

"No. I mean, I don't have any plans. I thought I might go for a swim."

Keith grinned. "I bought this inflatable boat thing from the big-box store on the highway. Want to come sailing with me?"

She sighed. She really didn't want to hang out with him and his frat-boy friends all week. Now might be the time to disconnect. She put on a polite smile, ready to tell him she wanted a little time alone, but then she noticed someone on the beach. It was a man, his dark hair whipped by the wind off the lake, his legs long and sleek in their familiar khaki cargo shorts. He was too far away for her to see his face clearly, but she could tell by his stance that he was staring at her. She'd recognize that lean runner's body anywhere.

She smiled and put a hand on Keith's arm. "That sounds like fun. You don't have anything reunion-y to do this morning?"

"Nah, we're on our own. A lot of guys' wives are making them go to some antique mall or something. Mike's going along to get something to take home to his old lady. Evidently, she likes some kind of pink glassware. I don't know what it is, but I started tuning out once they said antiques, you know?"

She laughed as if he had said something amusing, though she enjoyed antiques too. Aidan wouldn't be able to hear her, but he could see her.

"I think going out in your boat would be a lot more fun," she said. "Why don't you sit down and have some breakfast with me, and then I'll go up and get my hat and sunglasses."

"Yeah, sounds great." He glanced over at her plate. "Do you think they have something a little less fussy than those pancake things, whatever they are? Bacon and eggs or something?"

"I think the pancakes are delicious, but you can always ask Grace if there's something else. They're pretty accommodating here."

She nodded toward the door as Grace came in with her coffeepot. Madison was behind her.

"Good morning," Grace said to Keith. "Are you ready for breakfast?"

"Yeah," Keith said. "I was wondering if you have something less rich than the pancakes. Bacon or something? Cereal?"

"I could whip you up some scrambled eggs and sausage. And some wheat toast?"

"Perfect. Thank you."

Grace nodded. "Coming right up then. How about you, Madison? What would you like?"

"Just toast and coffee, thank you."

"Are you sure? You've probably got a big day ahead of you with the reunion. Don't you want a bigger breakfast?" There was a touch of concern in Grace's expression. "There's plenty of pancakes. Or I could make you eggs and sausage too. There's fruit if you'd like something lighter."

"I'd take some fruit, please, if you have it. No melon though."

"No melon." Grace smiled and poured her and Keith both a cup of coffee. Then she topped off Sarah's cup and went back into the inn.

"How are you two today?" Madison asked shyly.

"Doing okay," Keith said. "Where's Donny this morning?"

"I-I don't know. It's not like we actually know each other or anything." A dark flush rose into her cheeks.

"We're about to go rowing on the lake," Sarah said. "Would you like to come along?"

Keith glared at her over Madison's shoulder, but Madison only shook her head.

"Thank you, but I can't. I have an important letter to write this morning."

"Aww, that's too bad," Keith said, brightening. "Maybe next time."

"Yeah," Madison said.

Sarah watched as Madison busied herself adding cream and sugar to her coffee. She couldn't help thinking there was something going on between her and Donny, the guy in the loft. She didn't know much about softball, but from where she was sitting, she had been sure Madison had reached home before being tagged. *Stop it.* She had enough to keep herself occupied without taking on somebody else's issues.

She glanced up and saw that the beach across the lake was now unoccupied. Would Aidan be able to see her from his room when she was out on the lake with Keith? She hoped so.

Sarah didn't see Aidan on the beach again when she was out in the boat, but she couldn't be sure if he was watching or not, so she had to pretend she was enjoying her time with Keith. Obviously, the man thought he was God's gift to womankind, and he seemed especially impressed with his own faintly suggestive witticisms. Sometimes it was a challenge to turn the conversation back to something of a more innocent nature.

His boat was one of those little inflatable jobs with plastic paddles, barely big enough for two. She didn't know whether it was sturdy enough to last more than one summer, but it seemed like it would get them out onto the lake and back.

"Do you do much boating?" she asked, using one hand to keep her straw hat from being tugged off by the wind. Perhaps she ought to use that hatpin for something more than decoration.

He stopped paddling and let them drift for a while. "Not a whole lot actually, but I thought this would be a good way to spend some time with you without a lot of interruptions."

Inwardly, she sighed, but she forced a not-too-coy smile. "I thought you were here for the reunion."

"Yeah, but that'll be over tomorrow. A guy doesn't run into a looker like you every day."

What a line. She only barely managed not to roll her eyes. "Where'd you say you're from? California? I'm sure there are a lot of pretty girls there."

"Thousands," he said with a smirk, "but I've seen them all."

As if. "I haven't been there," she told him. "It must be nice to be that close to the ocean all the time. You must do all the water sports—surfing and snorkeling and swimming."

"Sure, everybody out there does, but I got a little bored with it, you know? I'm more into sailing now. Rafting's really my thing, to be honest. White-water rafting."

"Grace at the inn mentioned she enjoys kayaking," Sarah said. "That sounds fun."

"I guess, but you're stuck out there all by yourself. And if you turn over . . ." He made a face and shuddered.

This time she didn't have to manufacture a giggle. He loved white-water rafting but seemed reluctant to get wet. What was that about? He probably didn't do even half the things he claimed to. "I bet you—"

She caught a flicker of movement out of the corner of her eye. Aidan was there on the opposite shore. He had definitely seen them.

She leaned a little closer to Keith. "I bet you've done so many interesting things. I'd love to hear about them."

He reached over and tucked a strand of her hair behind her ear. "And I'd love to tell you about them," he murmured, leaning closer.

Seeing that Aidan had once more disappeared, she dipped her

fingers into the water and flicked them at Keith's face.

"Hey!"

"Are we going to sit here all day or see more of the lake?" she asked playfully. "If we're going to that drag race, we can't stay out here all day."

"Aww, that's not for hours yet. Don't be a spoilsport."

"I don't want to miss lunch either. Maybe we could go eat at The Tidewater later. I hear the food is wonderful."

Keith shrugged. "Yeah, sure. Why not? You are going to the race with me, right?"

"If you're a good boy."

"And the dance tomorrow night? That's the reunion's last event." He traced one finger along her nose and down to her lips. "I plan for you to be crazy about me by then. Just so you know."

"I see." She batted her lashes at him as if she thought he was only being silly. "I'll see if I can work that into my schedule."

He laughed and rowed farther down the shore.

They spent a while longer tooling around near the beach, watching the waterbirds and the little animals that lived there. Lunch at The Tidewater was delicious, but Sarah didn't catch even a glimpse of Aidan. When she and Keith returned to the inn, she found an envelope waiting for her at the front desk. It was addressed to her in Aidan's meticulous script and written on Tidewater stationery.

"He dropped it off while you were out," Grace told her. "I didn't know when you would be back in, so I told him it would be better if he didn't wait."

"Makes no difference to me."

Grace's eyes widened as Sarah ripped the still-folded note into halves, then quarters, then eighths. Then she dropped the pieces into the trash can.

Keith laughed and then headed up the stairs to his room.

"Don't you think you should at least see what he has to say?" Grace asked. "I know it's none of my business, but he obviously cares about you."

"I already know what he has to say. According to him, it's all my fault, even though he's the one who jilted me. What else is there to know?"

"I know it's not easy to find someone who really loves you." There was a touch of wistfulness in Grace's expression. "I had that once, and then I lost him. I've never found anyone yet who could take his place, and that was twenty-one years ago."

Sarah felt as if she'd been punched in the stomach. "I'm so sorry. What happened?"

"He was in a train accident. In Prague of all places." Grace's smile was in place, but smaller and sadder than usual. "He was there on business, and he never came home. Our little boy, Jake, was only three at the time."

"It must have been hard raising him alone," Sarah said.

"Sometimes," Grace admitted. "But I wouldn't have missed having him for anything in the world. And even though we had only a short time together, I've never been sorry I was married to Hank. He was one in a million. I'm not saying there could never be anyone else for me, but he'd have to be an awfully special man, and those don't come along every day."

"Or they don't come along at all," Sarah grumbled.

"No, they're out there. I'm sure of that. We just have to recognize them when we see them." There was a twinkle in Grace's eye as she glanced toward the stairs. "And be careful to not be taken in by cheap imitations."

Sarah shrugged. "If I can't have forever, I can at least have right now."

Grace winced but didn't say anything else. Yeah, well, Sarah didn't quite believe it either, but it sounded strong and independent, didn't it?

"I don't mean to intrude," Grace said, "but I felt so bad for him when he came and asked for you. I hope you can understand my concern. For you both."

"I do," Sarah said, "and I appreciate your advice, but I can handle this myself."

"Of course you can," Grace said, clearly not quite knowing what else to say. "Will you be joining us for hors d'oeuvres this evening?"

"I don't think so, thanks. I'm going with Keith to the drag races with the rest of the alums."

"All right. Let me know if there's anything I can do for you,"

With that, Grace disappeared into the kitchen. Sarah waited until she was sure her hostess wasn't coming back, then scooped the fragments of the note out of the trash can and bolted up to her room.

14

Grace

"I forgot to get avocados," Charlotte announced when Grace stepped into the kitchen.

Grace sighed, not really wanting to deal with something so insignificant right now. "Can we do without until tomorrow?"

"I can make tomorrow's mini beef Wellingtons for tonight and do the scallop-and-avocado tostadas tomorrow. After I go back to Hanson's. Again. I'm not sure why I didn't—" Charlotte broke off. "What's wrong?"

"Nothing, I guess." Grace sat at the table and started peeling the freshly boiled potatoes that were cooling there. "But I wonder if I ought to keep my mouth shut more times than not."

Winston trotted in and made himself comfortable at her feet. He could always sense when someone was upset and needed his soothing presence.

"Who is it this time?"

"Sarah, the would-be bride. Evidently her former groom is trying to work things out with her, but she's more interested in the guy up in Rosebud."

"I don't know." Charlotte took a variety of cheeses out of the refrigerator and started cutting them into bite-size cubes. "I think she's more interested in proving how much she doesn't care about the first guy. What's his name? Aidan?"

"Yes, I think so."

"She'd know best whether he deserves a second chance," Charlotte said, slicing through a piece of cheddar with quick, expert strokes. "Better than we would."

"I know." Grace got up to get a bowl for the peeled potatoes, careful not to disturb her already-drowsing dog. "Whatever he did, that doesn't mean she should be toying with the other guy like that."

"Rosebud?" Charlotte snickered. "A player if I ever saw one. He's been taking Dean Bradley lessons, if you ask me."

"Dean isn't that bad, is he?"

"I guess not. Or at least not as obvious."

"Well," said Grace, going back to peeling potatoes, "from what I can see, Keith just wants someone on his arm to impress his old school buddies. I'm not quite sure what Sarah wants from him except to feel admired and wanted again. That's pretty understandable after what she's been through, but neither of them is exactly full of consideration for the other. I hope she doesn't get herself in too deep."

"She's a big girl," Charlotte reminded her. "She can take care of herself."

"Yes, she made that very clear. I was only trying to help." Grace couldn't keep a bit of hurt out of her voice.

"You always do." Charlotte gave her an understanding smile. "She might have listened more than she let on."

"I hope so. It's hard for me to see someone hurting and not try to do something to make it better. And I guess it's like everything everybody does—we don't always see how what we say and do affects other people. For good or bad. So I guess I'll keep trying to do what I can."

"I can't imagine you doing anything else," Charlotte said. "It's like Aunt Winnie's little notions about when somebody needs a certain 'gift.' It's who she is."

Grace laughed softly. "I wonder what that hatpin was about."

"The one she gave Sarah?" Charlotte shook her head. "I don't know. I wish she'd give me something to help me figure out how to fix this rumor about my recipes."

"You never told me what your editor said."

"The good thing is that he wasn't as upset about it as I was afraid he was going to be. He told me the worst thing I could do would be to make a big deal about defending myself. That would only make people think there must be something to the rumors."

"Tristan has a lot of experience in publishing," Grace said. "I'm sure he knows best how to handle it. I'm sure that's why you're listening to him, though you wouldn't listen to me when I told you to let it blow over."

Charlotte gave her a sheepish grin. "I know, I know. You're always right and I should listen to you by now."

"As long as you realize that. He wasn't upset with you, was he?"

"No, thank goodness. He told me he knows I would never claim to have created a recipe that was someone else's, so at least he's in my corner. All he wants is for me to let him know if anything else happens."

"That sounds like a good strategy." Grace studied her sister for a minute. She did seem much calmer than before. "Does that mean you've given up on ripping into Dean and demanding a public apology?"

Charlotte stuck her nose in the air. "For now. But I reserve the right to change my mind."

Grace chuckled. "All right, Garbo, but remember you don't have the slightest bit of evidence against him."

"But it's him. I know."

"Like those people spreading rumors about your recipes 'know' you stole them?"

"Fine. Be rational." Charlotte got out a serving tray and began setting the cheeses on it in an artistic arrangement along with some water crackers and grapes.

"I think you need more evidence before you make any accusations. Tristan's right. Let it go for now. Don't make it worse by making a big deal out of it."

"Yes, yes, I know." Charlotte glanced at the clock over the sink. "Hey, would you do me a favor? Spencer was so nice to bring those pecans over the other day. I made some of that chicken salad he likes as a thank-you, and I thought maybe he'd want to have it for dinner. But if I take it over to the farm now, I won't get the flowers done and the mini beef Wellingtons made before six. I feel bad that I haven't done anything up until now, and I hate to wait any longer, especially since I want the chicken salad to be as fresh as possible when he gets it."

"I'll take it over. The rooms are all done, and Winston and I could use a little walk."

The dog popped his head up at the mention of his name and *walk*, and a couple of minutes later, he and Grace were on their way.

Blossom Hill Farm was only about half a mile down the lane from the inn. The white two-story farmhouse sat on the edge of a thirty-acre pecan orchard, peaceful and picturesque. Grace always enjoyed the walk out this way, and it was so much nicer now that the old house was no longer empty. And Winnie was right—she felt safer with someone like Spencer so close. He was proving to be a good neighbor and a good friend.

Bailey started barking the minute she knocked, and Winston was quick to respond. A moment later, Spencer opened the door and smiled to see her.

"Grace. And Winston too. How are you both? Come in."

He silenced his dog, who was straining to get to Winston, and then stepped back to let Grace in, but she only shook her head.

"I really can't stay. We're only out for our walk, but Charlotte sent you this." She handed him the container of chicken salad. "We're both so happy to have the pecans you brought over the other day. You'll have to come try a slice when she makes her chocolate pecan pie with them. You'll never eat regular pecan pie again."

"I don't know," he said with feigned skepticism. "I love regular pecan pie."

"So do I, but this is better. You wait and see."

"It's a date then," Spencer said. "So, what's this?" Before she could answer, he took the lid off the container, and his eyes widened. "Is this her world-famous chicken salad?"

"I don't know about world-famous, but it is delicious. She knows it's a favorite of yours."

"It definitely is. Please thank her for me." He replaced the lid. "Hey, since you're here, I have a question for you."

"Ask away."

"Have you started renting out inflatable boats?"

Grace laughed. "No way. If it's the one I'm thinking of, it's definitely not property of the Magnolia Harbor Inn. But why do you ask?"

"For one thing, it didn't look like much of a boat, and the guy paddling it didn't look like much of a sailor." Spencer seemed mildly disgusted. "What a hot dog."

"You know how guys like that are when they want to impress someone."

"I would have been more impressed if he had been smart enough to wear a life jacket. Him and the woman he was with."

"I did suggest it before they went out on the lake, but he didn't seem worried about it. He told me they weren't going far."

"People drown even when they're not going far," Spencer said, and his expression was stern.

"I'll suggest it again if they go back out, but I'm not sure they will. Either way, he's leaving Sunday. He's here for a class reunion. They have a lot of activities planned, so he might not have time for boating again."

"Good to know." Spencer's expression lightened. "And it's good of you to try to get them to be safe, whether or not they actually did what you suggested."

"Yes, I'm full of good suggestions that nobody pays attention to."

"I'm sure that's not true. Not all the time anyway." He gave her a wry smile. "Not for somebody who cares about people as much as you do."

His comment made her face feel warm. "Why do you say that?"

"I know I haven't known you that long, but I can tell. I can tell from what everybody in Magnolia Harbor says about you, and by how you treat the people you're around. If some of them aren't smart enough to know that, their loss, right?"

"Maybe I need you to write me a press release. 'If Grace Porter gives you life advice, you should listen. She's doing it for your own good.' Just so people will know."

"I might do exactly that." There was warmth in his blue eyes. "Are you sure you both can't come in for a minute? Bailey would love to have some company."

The dog wagged her tail at the mention of her name, bright-eyed and eager. She was nine years old, but she didn't act a day over six months.

"I can't stay. It'll be time for hors d'oeuvres before I know it." Grace leaned down and ruffled the thick fur on top of the dog's head. "I'm sorry, honey, but you and Winston can play another time."

"Tell Charlotte thank you for me," Spencer reminded her. "I know exactly what I'm having for dinner now."

"That's what she was hoping. Well, I'd better be getting back."

"See you soon."

She turned and waved when she got to the lane. "Thank you for the pecans—from both of us."

"You're both welcome," he called back, and she was aware that he continued to stand there on the porch until a bend in the lane took them out of sight.

15

Sarah

The note lay in eight pieces on top of the dresser in Sarah's suite—eight nearly identical squares of paper with Aidan's distinctive writing on them. His letters slanted when he was in a hurry. Or upset.

Dear Sarah,

You know I'm not a pushy guy. I figure if someone doesn't want to be with me, then it's better for both of us if we're apart. But I also figure that what we had—what we could still have—is worth fighting for. That doesn't mean anything if you don't feel the same way, though. It doesn't mean anything if you won't hear me out and at least try to understand. I know the wedding was important to you. I know it was something you had always wanted. I realize it's a very emotional time for a bride. All I asked was for you to slow down a little, for you to be sure I was the one, but you blew up at me. I don't know what you're thinking now, if you're only playing with that other guy or what, but I'd like for us to talk. And I mean seriously talk. Could we do that? I know your reservation is through Sunday. So is mine here at The Tidewater. If you want to try again, let me know. I still love you—the girl I met six-and-a-half months ago, the girl I fell head over heels in love with—but if I don't hear from you before I leave Sunday, then I'll know you would rather leave things as they are, and I won't bother you again.

Aidan

P.S. I sent your dad a check to cover the reception we didn't have. He hasn't cashed it yet.

Dad. Wonderful Dad. He had saved for her wedding ever since she was a little girl playing in a beat-up pair of white satin heels and a cheap bride costume leftover from Halloween. He had put away money, bit by bit, for her college and for her wedding, and she had made sure to tell him as the years went on what she had envisioned having and what it was likely to cost. And if he had to make his car or his golf clubs do for an extra year or two, he had never complained.

Sarah thought back on it now. Perhaps she could have planned a more modest wedding and reception and left the rest for her parents to do something they would have enjoyed. They had been married in the front room of their pastor's home with only their own parents and their best man and maid of honor. Then they had moved into the little house Dad had bought for them, and that was that. Their marriage was what mattered to them, not the wedding.

Jenny Cavalari, her matron of honor, had teased her about expecting her father to pay for her wedding and reception at her age. Sarah had snapped at her. She had waited for this all her life. She had dreamed and planned. He had saved that money for her. Why shouldn't he pay for it? Why should it matter if she was thirty now and not twenty-one? Why should she still have to be tormented by everyone simply because she was still not married?

The memory made her feel a little sick. She had almost lost her best friend over it. She had lost her groom. And she certainly hadn't looked good doing it.

She sat on the bed, staring at nothing. Why couldn't they see? All her friends had married years before. Whether or not those couples were still together wasn't the issue. They'd had their day. Why shouldn't she have hers? Why should she be the only one left behind? If Aidan really loved her like he said he did, he would have understood that. He wouldn't have humiliated her the way he had the moment people were finally through talking about poor single Sarah.

She crumpled up the carefully arranged pieces of his note and marched them into the bathroom. A moment later they were swirling down into the sewer.

She had a drag race to go to.

Madison

"Poor Marvin?" Kim asked with a giggle. "Why in the world would you ask about him?"

Madison looked around the restaurant they had chosen for lunch before the reunion dance, hoping no one she knew had overheard. Kim had never quite grasped the concept of subtlety. Emma and Kathy giggled along with her. They all might be thirty-two and not seventeen anymore, but they hadn't changed much. Kathy was still perfectly groomed, smart and steely. Emma was still cute and curly-topped, feminine and casual all at once. Kim was still a bright-eyed little pixie with black hair always in a ponytail to her waist. Madison could still picture them all by the lockers in the main hall.

Kathy patted her short, ultra-chic, blonde-tipped hair. "I haven't kept up with anyone from high school. It was hard enough getting away from the office for this little collegiate get together. And I certainly didn't keep up with Poor Marvin."

"Try getting away when you have a couple of kids," Emma groused.

"One's bad enough," Kim chimed in, "especially when you have a husband who never changed a diaper or put a baby to bed in his whole life. He's probably calling his mother thirty times a day until I get back."

Kathy made a wry face. "That's not as bad as being *married* to the baby. I thought Andre was going to burst into tears when I told him I'd be away for a few days and he'd have to figure out his own meals."

"So, you haven't married," Emma said, eyeing Madison as if she were some rare and faintly odorous species of fish. "But then you were always so intent on being the best at everything—music and scholastics and community service. It's no wonder you never had time for anyone."

Kim batted her long, inky lashes innocently. "Don't tell us you've been pining for Poor Marvin all these years."

Madison managed a hollow echo of everyone else's laugh. "Hardly. I was only curious. He kind of disappeared after we graduated high school. I thought I'd see him around at college, but I never did. Not in any of the arts programs anyway."

"I bet he didn't go." Kathy leaned conspiratorially closer to the other three. "At least, I bet he didn't graduate. He couldn't afford our school anyway, and then something happened to his mother. I don't know if she was sick or what, but he had to take care of her."

"She probably got a good look at Poor Marvin," Kim said, "and had to be put in an asylum."

"You're awful," Kathy said, laughing all the same.

Madison forced another tight smile. She wasn't going to tell them about Marvin's mother. She couldn't admit that she knew anything.

"Behave," Emma said with another giggle. "But I think he did go to our school. Remember that guy I went out with a couple of times in our sophomore year? Alvin?"

"Oh, yeah," Kim said. "Alvin and the Chipmunks, his little role-playing buddies. Saw them at the what-a-drag race last night. I'm sure he misses you to this day." She smirked.

Emma put her hands on her hips. "You're never going to let me live him down, are you? Anyway, he was a business major, and he knew Poor Marvin, so Poor Marvin must have been in school then. Don't know if he graduated, and I sure wasn't going to start asking around for Alvin at the reunion."

"You never know," Madison said, putting a little more tartness into her voice than she probably should have. "Could be that now Alvin owns a multimillion-dollar gaming software company and is married to a supermodel."

Emma snorted but didn't argue.

"I shouldn't laugh at Alvin," Kim said, a wicked gleam in her eye, "because I remember when Kathy almost married Ralph Bemenderfer!"

She and Emma shrieked with laughter, and Kathy gave them both a poisonous glare.

"I did not 'almost marry' him. We were set up on a blind date, and I think you two had your nasty little fingerprints all over that one. I bailed as soon as I could and had to dodge his calls for a month, you creeps. Anyway . . ."

Madison tuned them out, thinking back instead on the note she had left in the hatbox the morning after the softball game. Yesterday morning.

I've tried to forgive her, she wrote. *I've tried to excuse that girl who was so cruel and thoughtless. I've told myself she was too afraid to do anything else at the time, that she was too young to really know how hurtful she was being. But I know that will never be enough until I can get Marvin to forgive her. To forgive me. Tomorrow's the reunion dance. If I can't find out any other way, I'm just going to ask some people there if they know anything about him. If they know how I can reach him. I can't care what they think about it anymore, and I don't deserve to be that prideful anyway. And if he's there, I'm going to tell him I'm sorry. If he wants to make a fool of me then, at least it will be the end of the reunion. At least I won't have to face anyone from college ever again.*

That tomorrow was today. The dance was today. If Marvin wasn't there, surely someone would know how to get in touch with him, someone from accounting or engineering or wherever else his kind hung out. *His kind.* She cringed inwardly. As if she and "her kind"—girls like Kathy and Kim and Emma—were somehow inherently superior to the less gifted, the less secure, the less elegant. Perhaps they were lovely on the outside, but she knew from personal experience that that didn't guarantee a beautiful inside.

"Earth to Madison!"

Madison blinked as Kim snapped her fingers under her nose.

"Is anybody in there?"

"Sorry." Madison shrugged a little. "What did you say?"

"We were asking about your dress for tonight," Kathy said. "Mine's only a little Vera Wang sheath in slate shantung. Kim says hers is a white strapless. And, well, after two babies, Emmie had to settle for something not quite so formfitting."

Emma chuckled. "The babies have nothing to do with it, thank you. I happen to like a full skirt. It reminds me of something Grace Kelly might have worn back in the day."

"*After* she had her children," Kim put in.

"Droll. Very droll."

"What else is yours like?" Madison asked Emma.

"Pale pink with a sweetheart neckline. What about yours?"

"Umm . . ." Madison began, trying to think of how to describe her dress.

"You are going, aren't you?" Kathy asked.

Madison felt slightly nauseated. This was it. Tonight she faced the music.

"Going?" She forced a bright smile. "Of course I am."

17

Charlotte

Coffee. Charlotte made a snap decision as she noticed the Dragonfly Coffee Shop across the street. She had picked up her dry cleaning and Grace's, bought vacuum cleaner bags and furniture polish, retrieved a package from the post office and been disappointed that it was not copies of her last cookbook from Chow Bella, and remembered to get avocados for that evening's hors d'oeuvres. After all that, she deserved—no, *needed* a decadent cup of specialty coffee. A classic vanilla latte ought to do the trick.

She packed all her burdens into her black Camry and headed across to the coffee shop.

"Hey, Charlotte."

Angel Diaz smiled at her from behind the counter. She was an artist when she wasn't working part-time at the coffee shop, and Charlotte never knew what whimsical little touches she might be sporting despite the demure blue apron that was part of her usual uniform. Today she had a tiny butterfly tattooed beside her left eye. It was one of those temporary ones, but combined with Angel's brown eyes, olive skin, and jet-black hair, it gave her an exotic and Bohemian appearance.

Charlotte hurried over to her. At the moment, there was no one else in the shop. Maybe now was a good time for Charlotte to find out who had been talking about her and her recipes.

"What'll it be today?" Angel asked.

"I think a large vanilla latte."

"And lots of whipped cream," Angel added. "Coming right up."

She bustled around behind the counter, and Charlotte heard the hiss of steamed milk mixed with espresso.

"I was wondering if you've heard anything about my recipes recently," Charlotte said, trying to sound casual.

"I didn't hear anything directly. There were a couple of ladies in here talking, and then Mrs. Abrams really tore into them about it. She told them that if you said you made up a recipe, then you made it up, and that was that. The two ladies started arguing with her, so I told them I knew the same as Mrs. Abrams and I didn't want to hear any more about it, either in here or around town. It's ridiculous what people will say when there's no real news talk about."

Charlotte's cheeks were warm now. "You don't know what they said?"

"I'm afraid not."

"Who was it?"

Angel shook her head. "I don't think you need to worry about that. After Mrs. Abrams was through with them, I don't think they ever wanted to spread gossip in Magnolia Harbor again."

"I didn't believe a word of it!"

Startled, Charlotte turned to see a petite redhead in skinny jeans and a navy-and-white-striped knit top standing behind her.

"Laurie, hi! I didn't hear anyone come in."

"You two were talking, and I didn't want to interrupt, but you should know I'm on your side. Gotta stand up for my old work buddy, right?"

"How are you?" Charlotte asked with a smile.

"I'm so good," Laurie said. "I was going to get an espresso. Want to sit down for a minute?"

"Sure. Great." Charlotte definitely wanted to know what Laurie had heard and from whom. "I already ordered mine. Why don't you go ahead, and I'll get us a table."

"I'll bring your drinks over when they're ready," Angel said.

"Thanks."

Charlotte chose the little corner table farthest from the counter. If anyone else came in, she didn't want to be overheard. She couldn't believe Laurie Mason had come here. Charlotte hadn't even thought of her in a long time. Laurie had worked at *Le Crabe Fou* with Charlotte—and Dean. Laurie had been the hostess, and she had certainly looked stunning in the quintessential little black dress all the hostesses wore. What in the world was she doing here in Magnolia Harbor?

"It's so good to run into you." Laurie tossed her little beaded bag on the table and sat down across from Charlotte. "It seems like ages. What have you been doing with yourself? I hear you have a bed-and-breakfast of your very own and the most fabulous line of cookbooks. That's awesome."

"I don't know if I'd call it a fabulous line, but I have had a few published. It's been a lot of fun. How did you hear about the inn?"

"You know, word gets around. And Dean mentions you now and then."

"Dean? You mean Dean Bradley, right?"

"Who else? You know we were kind of a thing back at the Crab."

Charlotte hadn't actually known that, but she managed to smile politely.

"We've been seeing each other off and on since he left there," Laurie went on, "so I hear about what goes on here in Magnolia Harbor. About The Tidewater and other things. You know how Dean is—always trying to impress. But you have to put up with a little bit of that with a man who's that delicious, right?"

"I haven't forgotten," Charlotte said, sidestepping the question. And she certainly remembered how he was—then and now.

"Anyway, I hope you're not too upset with him. I'm sure he doesn't mean any real harm, but he does sometimes say things he shouldn't. It's just the way he is. Like I said, I don't believe a word of it."

Charlotte sat staring at her. She had known that it was Dean. She had known it all along. Why did it sting so much to have it confirmed?

"One vanilla latte and one espresso," Angel said, setting down one steaming cup and then another. "Anything else?"

"We're good," Laurie said. "Thanks."

Angel returned to the counter.

"What exactly are you talking about?" Charlotte said, forcing her voice to stay low and even.

"Wasn't that what you two were talking about when I came in?" Laurie asked, her nut-brown eyes wide. "That nasty rumor about your recipes?"

"Yes, we were. I was only trying to get to the bottom of it, and I had heard someone was talking about it in here recently. Are you sure Dean started it?"

"I'm afraid so," Laurie said, and she took a sip of her espresso. "This is fabulous. I'll definitely have to have him bring me here sometime soon."

Charlotte took her latte in both hands but didn't drink. "Why would he say something like that?"

Laurie gave her a sympathetic look. "I'm sorry, but I don't know. I overheard him talking to a couple in the dining room at The Tidewater. They were asking what he served for breakfast, and the wife mentioned she had heard how delicious breakfast was at your place. Well, Dean gave her that smug little smile of his—that cute little sly one, you know—and told her most of what she'd heard was only talk and that your signature dishes weren't all that original. I don't remember exactly what he said. It's not like he said it straight out, but he definitely gave her the impression that you had gotten your best ideas from him when you both worked at the Crab. I scolded him about it after that couple left, but he told me it was nothing but talk and I shouldn't worry about it." Laurie took another sip of her drink. "I thought about coming straight to you at the time, to let you know, but then I thought it would be better to keep quiet about it. I mean, isn't the best way to stop a rumor to simply let it die of loneliness? I had no idea that couple would blab."

"Right," Charlotte murmured. "Right."

"Anyway, I'm sorry it's been spread all over now. I ought to be furious with him over it, but I can never seem to be upset with him for long. Not with that beautiful face of his."

Charlotte swallowed a scalding mouthful of latte. Maybe Laurie wouldn't have found him so forgivably beautiful if she knew he had hired a matchmaker to find the right girl for him. A girl that wasn't Laurie.

"I didn't realize he was seeing anyone," Charlotte said coolly. "But then again, it's not like I catch more than a glimpse of him now and then in town."

"We're only off and on. You know how guys are. Lately more on than off though." Laurie's brown eyes sparkled. "So, who knows?"

She was certainly welcome to him, the snake.

"And what have you been up to?" Charlotte asked, not remotely interested in the answer. "Still working in Charleston?"

"I'm at the Omni now. Still hostessing, but I'm kind of managing the place, scheduling waitstaff and breaking up fights in the kitchen, working with vendors and all that kind of stuff." She giggled. "Not that they pay me for that, but the actual manager couldn't get along without me. One of these days, he's going to have to pay up or run the place by himself. I told him—" She glanced at her watch and then gasped. "I'm so sorry. I didn't realize what time it is, and I'm working tonight." She stood up and slung her bag over one shoulder. "It was so good to see you again. If you and whoever you're seeing come by the Omni some night for dinner, ask for me. I'll make sure you get our best table. Laters!"

She picked up her drink, wiggled her fingers in Charlotte's direction, and dashed out of the shop. Charlotte could only blink after her. Laurie always had been a whirlwind of activity, but if she had been trying to make Charlotte jealous, it wasn't working. She was welcome to Dean and his beautiful face. If he had any face left after Charlotte was finished with him.

She took several calming sips of her drink, watching as two couples came in and placed their orders, but she wasn't really seeing them. A glance at her own watch told her it was early enough for her to make a brief stop at The Tidewater before she had to get back to the inn. The stop might be brief, but she'd make sure it was memorable.

Madison

E*au de nil.* Water of the Nile. That's what they called the soft, blue-green color of the watered silk dress Madison was going to wear for tonight's dance. She had loved the dress from the moment she saw it in the window of the exclusive little shop a few blocks down from her office. Its classic lines and beautiful construction gave her somewhat-straight figure a little curve. Hopefully wearing it would make her feel beautiful inside too. The thought of it made her feel queasy. If she wore it, she'd have to go. If she went, she'd have to do what she had promised she'd do. She'd have to ask about Poor Marvin. She'd have to find someone who knew where he was and how to reach him.

She wouldn't worry about that quite yet. For now, she had something else to take care of. She picked up the plastic-sheathed Rangers uniform shirt she had just gotten back from the cleaners. It wasn't as if she had actually gotten it dirty wearing it from the softball game to the inn. And it wasn't as if it hadn't already been grubby from Donny wearing it during the game itself, but she couldn't return it to him unless it was in pristine condition. It was little enough to do to thank him for shielding her from embarrassment.

He'd been so kind that she had wished since then that she had the courage to talk to him about her problem. What a relief it would have been to tell someone, anyone, what had weighed her down all these years. But she couldn't tell him something like that. She still didn't know what he did for a living. Something creative, she was sure of that, something high-class and professional. He wouldn't want to hear about her high school angst, not when he barely knew her in the first place. Perhaps he was attracted to her, a little bit anyway. A tearful confession about Poor Marvin would be a sure way to snuff that out for good.

She wouldn't think about Poor Marvin or the dance or humiliating herself quite yet. She would go return Donny's Rangers jersey and thank him again for being so nice. It would be her last chance before the reunion was over.

She studied her appearance in the mirror one last time. She was still dressed for her lunch with the girls, her white capri pants and striped linen shirt casual but cute. It was exactly the right look for dropping by Donny's for a minute. She touched on a bit of lip gloss, picked up the hanger with the jersey on it, and headed up to the loft.

She hesitated once she got to the third floor of the inn. Perhaps this wasn't a good idea after all. She didn't want to give him the wrong impression or anything. Still, it wasn't as if she was going to invite herself in. She'd return the jersey and go back to her own room, simple as that. After that, she'd take a nice, leisurely bath and possibly a nap, and then get ready for the dance. No, she wouldn't think about the dance quite yet. She'd return the jersey and then worry about tonight later on. She didn't have to set right more than one thing at a time.

There were two doors there at the top of the stairs. One was marked *Staff Only*. That must be the attic. The other door led to the *Wisteria Loft Suite*. To Donny's room. She lifted her chin and gave the door three solid raps. When there was no immediate response, her nerve left her. She wouldn't wait. He was probably out anyway. She'd hang the jersey on the doorknob and be done with it. If she saw him around later, she'd thank him for his help. That would be good enough.

She had no more than reached toward the doorknob when the door opened. Donny stood there in sweatpants, a T-shirt, and socks, apparently half asleep and a little bewildered. He had a copy of *Crime and Punishment* under his arm.

"Madison," he said, and his voice was even deeper than usual. "Sorry. I guess I dozed off reading."

"I'm sorry I woke you." She held up the jersey. "I only wanted to bring this back and tell you again how much I appreciate your help."

"Not a problem. It wasn't much."

"It meant a lot to me," she said.

He ducked his head a little, an almost shy gesture that seemed somehow familiar. Had she seen him around college all those years ago? Surely she'd have remembered him. But she hadn't known a Donny then. She was sure of it.

"You didn't need to have this cleaned," he told her. "It's pretty beat-up already. I would have just taken it home and tossed it into the wash with everything else."

"That wouldn't have been very polite, especially after you'd been so nice and kept me from being humiliated in front of the whole class."

There was a sudden grim wryness in his face. "That's never fun."

Maybe it was the thought of being humiliated at school that triggered her sudden thought. It could have been his stoic expression and the fleeting pain in his eyes. Heaven help her, she had seen those eyes.

"Do I know you?"

"No," he said gravely. "I don't think you ever did."

Sudden dread welled up inside her. It couldn't be.

It was.

God help her, she was going to be sick. The whole scene materialized before her in perfect clarity.

She was standing in front of her locker, checking her lip gloss and listening to Emma gush about the football player she was suddenly infatuated with. Kim was doing her best to scribble down a copy of the notes Kathy had taken in the biology class that Kim had spent doodling a barely recognizable sketch of her latest movie star crush with an extremely idealized version of herself. Kathy, meanwhile, was making arch comments on the clothing worn by the students who passed by them.

"Come on," Madison said, grabbing her books and slamming shut the locker door. "I can't be late to Goldman's class." She glanced up at the hall clock as she hurried away. "Last time I—"

She crashed straight into a boy coming the opposite way down the hall. The impact knocked the breath out of her and sent her glasses and both of their books flying. Only his steadying hand kept her from ending up on the painted cement floor.

"I'm sorry," she said, half blind now. "I wasn't paying attention."

The boy scooped up her glasses before they could be crushed by other kids hurrying to class and handed them to her. "It's okay."

Oh no. That gawky frame, that squeaky voice, it couldn't be—

"Isn't that sweet?" Kathy said, her syrupy voice exactly loud enough to carry throughout the hallway. "Madison and Poor Marvin."

Two boys from the basketball team snickered at her, and Madison glared back. Marvin kept his head down as he started picking up books.

She grabbed two of hers out of his hands. "I'll do it."

"Sure," he murmured, still looking down and then catching his own glasses before they slipped off his nose. "Sorry."

"Young love," Kim said with a smirk. "Touching."

His jaw clenched tight, Marvin snatched up his own books and bolted down the hall. A second later the bell rang.

"At least," Kathy said sweetly, "you'll have a good story to tell Mr. Goldman."

"Shut up," Madison hissed. "Just shut up."

"It's not the first time you've run into him accidentally on purpose," Kim teased.

"He can't help it if he's crushing on Madison," Emma said.

"He is not." Madison's voice broke and her eyes stung. She wouldn't cry. She wouldn't. That would only give them

more fodder. "I have to go. I'm late already."

"Don't be mad, Mad," Kathy called after her. "We won't tell anybody."

Their low laughter followed her down the hall.

She could still hear it now, here in the stark silence at the door of the Wisteria Loft Suite. She finally raised her head. He stood watching her, his expression completely unreadable.

She had to get out.

Without another word, she turned and bolted down the stairs, down to the second floor, down to the first. She couldn't possibly show her face inside the inn ever again. At least not to him.

She'd go out to the lake. She had seen a magnolia tree that was shady and secluded. Maybe that would be a good place to catch a breath of fresh air, to slow the racing of her heart. She sprinted to that tree and threw herself down at the base of it.

"God help me," she breathed. "God forgive me. What do I do? What do I do?"

She still couldn't believe it. Donny couldn't possibly be Poor Marvin. Poor Marvin was skinny and awkward. He wore thick glasses and had a squeaky voice and—

"I'm not sixteen anymore."

At the sound of his voice, Madison put both hands over her face and curled herself against the tree. "Go away. Please just go away."

He didn't say anything. He didn't go away.

Madison finally met his gaze, and then the tears began welling up. "Please," she breathed, the word hardly intelligible. "Please."

That unreadable expression was still on his face. "Didn't you want to tell me something?"

Charlotte

"Laurie Mason," Charlotte fumed as she pulled her black Camry into a parking spot in front of The Tidewater. She didn't know why she was so mad at Laurie right now. Probably because she had tried to excuse Dean's jerkiness even when Dean was clearly being a jerk to her too. Women like Laurie were the reason guys like Dean kept on being jerks. Well, Charlotte wasn't one of those. She wasn't going to let him keep doing whatever he wanted. Not at her expense.

She killed the engine, snatched her purse out of the front seat, and strode into the lobby, every sharp click of her heels the tick of a clock running out. The woman behind the desk greeted her professionally.

"I need to speak to Mr. Bradley," Charlotte said.

"Mr. Bradley is—"

"Don't tell me he's not here. I saw his car out front."

"He's in his office, ma'am. May I give him your name?"

Charlotte exhaled and softened her expression. "Yes, please. I'm Charlotte Wylde. And, yes, he knows me very well."

The woman nodded. "One moment, please." She picked up her phone and made a quick call.

A few seconds later, Dean came into the lobby. "Charlotte, I didn't expect to see you, especially here. Is there something I can do for you?"

She pursed her lips. "Besides jump in the lake?"

He glanced at the woman behind the desk again. She was attempting to rearrange the ballpoint pens in the little cup beside her computer and managing to knock most of them under the desk as she tried to pretend she wasn't eavesdropping.

"Would you like to come into the office?" Dean asked coolly. "Then we won't be in anyone's way."

She agreed, and a moment later they were sitting in a rather small room that reflected the crisp, modern decor of the rest of the inn. Charlotte couldn't help but notice the organization on his desk. It was so like him to have everything perfectly in place. *Could he be more pretentious?*

"Coffee?" he asked, lifting the sleek carafe from the warmer on the credenza behind him.

"I'm not staying."

"Mind if I have some?" He gave her that insufferable smirk of his. "I might need something to settle my nerves."

She studied him coldly. "Go ahead, though I've never heard that coffee helps with a guilty conscience."

The smirk vanished. "Hey, I told you I didn't have anything to do with that so-called date of ours. The matchmaker didn't tell me anything about who I'd be meeting, only that we were a great match." He refilled the coffee cup on his desk and replaced the carafe. "But don't worry, I already canceled all that. If you want to try again, you won't have to worry about me being in the pool of options."

"I didn't come to talk to you about that," she said. "In fact, right now dating is the last thing I want to bother with."

"And the male population of South Carolina breathes a sigh of relief."

"Really?" she asked, her blood coming dangerously close to a boil. "That's where you want to go right now?"

"Okay, okay, I'm sorry." He held up both hands in surrender. "You know I'm a smart aleck, but I'll try to behave. What's the problem now? You don't want me to refund the gas you used to get to Turner's, do you?"

She sat there, stone-faced, until she was sure he had finished talking. "This is not about the date. This is about you spreading lies about me all over town."

"Lies?" He frowned. "What lies?"

"Don't act like you don't know. You never were a very good liar, despite all the practice you've had."

His dark eyes turned icy. "I'm pretty busy right now. If you have something to say to me, then go ahead. I don't have time to guess what it is."

"Okay, I'll say it straight out. Stop telling people I stole my signature recipes. It's not true, as you are very well aware. And just so you know, I'm not going anywhere. The Magnolia Harbor Inn isn't going anywhere. I know you'd like to see us shut down so The Tidewater will have a monopoly in the area, but it's not going to happen. And I already talked to my editor at Chow Bella. He doesn't believe your lies, so doing this isn't helping your chances of getting in with them. As a matter of fact, if I told them precisely who was trying to sabotage me, that would end any hope you'd ever have of them offering you a contract for your cookbooks." She leaned a little further across the desk. "Ever."

His expression had grown colder and colder as she spoke. "May I speak now?" he asked, his tone clipped.

"Go ahead."

"First off," he said, "I have not been spreading rumors about you. Not about your recipes or about your inn or about anything at all. I'd like to know what proof you have that I've ever done anything like that."

"Come on," she said, feeling a little foolish all of a sudden. "Who else would do it?"

"So, I'm guilty because you can't think of anybody else to blame?" He lifted his eyebrows expectantly.

"Who do you think would do it?" she demanded.

He shrugged. "I don't have a clue. I only know it wasn't me. For one thing, I know you created those recipes yourself. I was at *Le Crabe Fou* when you came up with several of them."

She glared at him. "Knowing the truth wouldn't stop you from spreading a lie."

"A lot of other people were there too," he reminded her. "Why would I spread a rumor that could be so easily disproved?"

"Sometimes just the suspicion is enough to do the damage," she said, her mouth in a stubborn line.

"Exactly who told you about this anyway?"

"Normally I don't like to name names," Charlotte said, "but your girlfriend told me you didn't mean any actual harm."

"My girlfriend?"

If nothing else, the man was a good actor. Charlotte would have sworn he was genuinely surprised.

"Okay," she conceded, "I realize you're only off and on, but yeah, she did."

"I don't mean to be rude," he said, oozing artificial affability, "but are you out of your mind? What girlfriend?"

Charlotte huffed. "It's so childish of you to make me say it. Laurie Mason."

Dean groaned. "I should have known. I guess that explains everything."

Charlotte narrowed her eyes. "What do you mean?"

"Listen to me," he said, "and I want you to pay very close attention. Laurie and I are not dating. Not off and on. Not now and then. Not by any stretch of the imagination. If anyone is spreading rumors about you, my money would be on her."

"Why would she do something like that? I don't understand."

He picked up his coffee cup, not meeting her eyes. "I, uh, I guess it's because of me."

She bit back a cutting remark about his conceit, remembering how Laurie had talked about him.

"What do you mean?" she asked instead, though she had already guessed.

"I suppose you didn't notice it when we all worked at the Crab. She was always trying to get my attention. Trying too hard, if you ask me, and the harder she tried, the more of a turnoff it was. I wasn't ever anything but polite to her. I've seen her around Magnolia Harbor once or twice. She came in here a few times, and I treated her to coffee a couple of mornings because we used to work together. That's it. That doesn't qualify as dating, even off and on."

"No," Charlotte said reluctantly. "I guess not. And, to be honest, I did notice her trying to get your attention when we all worked together, but I thought you didn't want to mix business and personal relationships."

There was a touch of an ironic smile on his face, though she didn't know why. "As you might remember, that's a policy I've been trying my best to follow for quite a while, but in her case, that wasn't the reason. She was always too pushy for me. If there's any chasing to be done, I prefer to be the one doing it. But I like it best when it happens naturally, without any chasing at all." He ran one hand through his thick hair. "Man, I don't know what to say about this rumor thing. I can't tell you it's Laurie for certain, but she'd be my guess. I can also tell you, absolutely and in all sincerity, that it wasn't me."

She gave him a hard look, but he only stared back at her, with equal parts annoyance and openness. Well, maybe she'd be annoyed, too, if someone barged into the inn and made a lot of unproven accusations, especially if her last meeting with that person had ended as acrimoniously as her blind date with Dean had.

"Anything else you'd like to accuse me of?" he asked finally.

She huffed.

"May I ask a question or two of my own?" He refilled his coffee cup. "I didn't get much of a chance to respond to your . . . comments at Turner's the other night."

There was a sudden burning in her cheeks. She had been awfully waspish that night. "Go ahead."

"Thanks," he said. "And to show there's no hard feelings, I'll actually let you tell me your side of it when I'm done."

She clenched her jaw, knowing it was the only way to hold her tongue.

"For one thing, you accused me of trying to ruin you with Chow Bella. I don't know why you'd say that. Yes, I've sent them a couple of proposals for books featuring my Busy Man recipes, but how does that affect what you're doing with them? Busy men who don't know much about cooking aren't your target market, are they?"

"No, not exactly. But when you told me you were querying them about your manuscript when we still worked together, you said you were going to make sure they never gave me another contract."

"Charlotte!" He stared at her incredulously. "Is that what you heard? I admit I was being snarky. You had just told me in no uncertain terms that ours was strictly a business relationship. But I did not say I was going to make sure Chow Bella never gave you another contract. How could I do that even if I wanted to?"

"Spreading rumors might be a start," she grumbled sulkily.

"If you'll think back to it, you might remember what I said was that I was going to write a book that would make them forget all about you and your stupid recipes. And, yes, I confess that I said 'stupid.' It was childish of me, and I'm sorry, but that was all I said. I never, ever threatened to ruin your relationship with them. Be fair."

She remembered that night. That was exactly what he had said, and she had said a few childish things then too. "I guess . . . I guess maybe I've remembered it wrong all this time."

"I know you think I'm the devil's next-door neighbor, but I wouldn't do something like that to anybody. I couldn't live with myself if I did."

She felt a sudden urge to giggle, as inappropriate as that would have been, at his description of her opinion of him. And he might be right.

"And then there's that bit about me building The Tidewater only to spite you." He looked absolutely bewildered. "I don't even know what to say about that one. Who in the world does that? You must think I have serious grudge issues."

The anger she had harbored against him for so long boiled back to the surface. "You knew Grace and I were opening a place on Lake Haven. You spent weeks pretending like you were interested in me to make me tell you about our plans. So you could steal them."

Tears burned into her eyes. That was what had hurt most all this time. He had flirted with her, acted like he was interested in her, when all he had really wanted was to snatch up any ideas he could turn to his own profit. It was insufferable.

"Okay," he said after a silent moment. "Having a lakeside inn was your idea to start with. But I had always wanted to have a restaurant. Ask my parents. When you started talking about your inn, I thought it sounded great, and I wanted that future for myself. I mentioned it to a friend of mine who wanted to invest in something like that, and this is where we ended up."

"You happened to end up eight miles away from where my inn was completely by accident?" She pursed her lips. "I see."

"I knew you were going to be on the lake, but that's not why I ended up here too. My partner already owned this property. Actually, it was something he inherited from his grandparents. It hadn't been worth much at the time, but the way property values have gone up, we decided there was no way we could afford a new location for our inn. Besides, is it so bad having us over here? Both our places are fairly small. I haven't noticed either of us having a hard time staying full. I'm totally booked this weekend, and I've heard you are too."

"I guess you're right about that much."

"A few of my guests have said they wouldn't have stayed at The Tidewater if they hadn't known part of their group could be over at your place. I bet you and Grace have been told the same thing."

"Yeah," she muttered.

"Okay then." He gave her a small smile. "So I'm not such a bad guy after all."

She didn't say anything, mad at herself for not being mad at him anymore.

"Maybe?" he prompted after a second or two.

She remembered another grievance. "What about my recipes? Don't give me some convoluted story about how you didn't steal them. Exactly how did you come up with those 'Tidewater' pork chops? I'd love to hear about your creative process."

He winced slightly. "Those were inspired by you. At least the way we sear them twice and use a special rub in between."

"And that special rub? I don't suppose it accidentally happens to be the exact recipe you sweet-talked out of me when we still worked together?"

He exhaled. "Not exactly, no, but there are a lot of similarities." He tried a winsome smile. "If it wasn't so delicious, I wouldn't have borrowed it from you."

"You mean you wouldn't have stolen it," she spat.

"All right, all right. I'm sorry. Do you want me to take it off the menu? I've been thinking I should for quite a while now. We haven't called them

'Tidewater Pork Chops' for a long time anyway, just 'Pork Chops.'"

"Why not?"

"I didn't think it was right. It makes it sound like we invented them or something."

"Yes," she said tightly. "It does."

"Like I said, I'm sorry. I shouldn't have used your ideas without your permission. My only excuse, and I realize it's not a very good one, is that at the time you had pretty much invited me to never speak to you again, so I figured it wouldn't be a good time to ask. There's nothing I can do but take them off the menu and ask you to forgive me. Would that work?"

"That would be a start," she said guardedly. It certainly was hard to keep up this level of righteous indignation when he was being so reasonable.

"All right, it's done. Will you please forgive me?"

"I don't think that will be necessary."

"What?"

"I mean taking them off the menu," she said, annoyed to feel heat in her cheeks. "And, yes, I do forgive you. The recipe thing was a long time ago, and I don't want to hang onto it anymore." She held out her hand. "Are we good?"

"Good." He shook her hand and then glanced at his watch. "Hey, I'm sorry, but I have a game to get to. I'm glad we've cleared the air, and if you want to talk more, let me know."

"A game?" She smiled a little. "I didn't know you played sports."

"Oh, I'm not playing. I help out with a Little League team. It's fun."

She didn't know why he should be shy about admitting he volunteered to help local kids, but that made it all the more appealing.

"That's nice," she said, "and, yeah, maybe we ought to talk again. Or better yet, we ought to talk to Laurie and find out exactly what she knows. Hopefully that will take care of things once and for all."

"Good idea," he said. "She deserves a chance to tell her side too, right?"

He gave her another of his wry grins, and this time she responded in kind.

"I guess. If we're going to be totally fair." She walked with him to the door and then stopped. "By the way, that was a little strange, the two of us being set up for a date."

He shrugged. "Not really. We're both about the same age, live in the same area, work in the hospitality industry. We even both write cookbooks."

"When you put it that way, I suppose it would have been strange if we hadn't been matched up. I'm surprised that you hired a matchmaker though. I would have thought you'd have women lining up." *Did I actually say that out loud? What is wrong with me?*

He chuckled. "Yeah right. Actually, I was running into too many girls like Laurie. And Laurie herself. But I think you and I should get to the bottom of this rumor thing with her so we can get back to finding someone who's right for each of us. When would be a good time?"

Charlotte frowned, thinking. "I don't know. I don't have any way to get in touch with her or anything. Do you?"

"She made sure I had her phone number," Dean said with a pained expression. "But I'd rather give you a call the next time she comes by. Then we can both talk to her."

"All right. That ought to be okay. As long as I'm not in the middle of something at the inn."

"We'll play it by ear," he said. "Deal?"

"Deal."

He walked her out to her car and opened the door for her to get in. "I'll let you know if I hear from her. Sometimes she calls or texts to see if I'm going to be around." He made another face.

"Got it," Charlotte said as she clicked on her seat belt. "Have fun at your game."

He beamed at her. "I always do."

She drove away wondering what she had gotten herself into.

20

Madison

"I thought you had something to tell me," Donny said when Madison merely stared up at him from the grass under the magnolia tree.

"Why do you call yourself Donny?" she asked finally, sniffing to keep her nose from running.

"My last name's Donovan, but I guess you wouldn't know that."

She said nothing. She knew, but she hadn't made the connection. He had always been nothing but Poor Marvin to her.

He sat on the grass beside her and gazed out over the lake.

"Why did you lend me your shirt?" she asked quietly. "Didn't you think a little dose of humiliation was exactly what I deserved?"

"Why would I want that? I know how it feels."

She peeked at him from under her lashes. He had always been tall, but it had been a geeky kind of tall, scrawny and awkward. He was still tall and slim, but it was the sleek, muscular slimness of a runner or a tennis player. The adolescent squeak in his voice had deepened into rich velvet, his glasses had been replaced by contacts or eliminated by laser surgery, and his teeth were straight and white.

But the eyes—oh, Lord help her, the eyes were the same. There was still a touch of raw emotion behind the impassivity there. If she had ever really seen him back then, it would never have taken her so long to recognize him now.

She sniffed, wishing she had a tissue or something. She couldn't bear the thought of embarrassing herself even more than she already had.

"Sorry," he said, still not looking at her. "I usually carry a handkerchief, but there aren't any pockets in these sweatpants."

Again, they were both silent. Evidently, he was okay with waiting there until she was ready to talk.

"You were the one who answered my notes," she said at last.

"Yeah."

"Donny—" Her throat tightened. "Marvin. I am so sorry about all of this. You don't know how awful I've felt all these years about what I did."

"Yeah, I do. I read your notes, remember?"

"I don't know what made me do it in the first place," she told him, and then she winced. Now wasn't the time to be dishonest with him or herself. "No, I do know. I wanted that music scholarship they were awarding our senior year, and I found out you had applied for it too. And then my mother found out from a friend of hers who worked at the school that it was down to you and me, so right before your audition, I sabotaged your trumpet."

She could still see him sitting there that day, fumbling through the piece he had been assigned to play, panic in his eyes as he licked his numb lips, inadvertently making his tongue go numb along with them. Her dad had played the trombone when he was in high school, and one time he had mentioned pranking other brass players by rubbing numbing gel on their mouthpieces. He would have been so ashamed of her if he had found out what she had done.

"It was awful. I didn't do anything but sit there and watch while you tried to play."

"I figured out what happened after a minute or two," he said. "No one had ever done it to me before. Most of the guys didn't bother with me, but I had seen it done a couple of times. I just couldn't believe you had done it. Especially right then."

She stared out over the lake, wishing she could dive in and never come back up. "Why didn't you tell someone what happened? They would have given you another chance."

"I didn't want to get you into trouble. All I wanted to do was get out of there and hide out at home. Mom wanted to call the school and set them straight, but I wouldn't let her. I told her I didn't deserve anything better." He chuckled. "She lit into me right then and there, and she was right. Whatever I made of myself, it was up to me and not anybody else. I'd get what I worked for, as long as I kept working for what I really wanted."

"I think if I had played my piano concerto after you, I would have flopped too. The minute you started playing, the minute I truly realized what I had done, I regretted it. I know you won't believe me now, but it's true. I wished I had left you alone, but it was too late."

"You might have said something then," he said, and his tone was as casual as if he were talking about the weather.

"That's what makes it worse. I didn't say anything. I didn't do anything. I just let it happen. I let you lose a scholarship I knew you needed, a scholarship I could easily have done without. My parents were well-off, and I knew you didn't have anyone but your mother. I knew it would be hard for you to get into college, especially our school, without a scholarship. I still let it happen. I ruined your whole future, and after all that, I ended up dropping music and majoring in art."

"Did you hate me that much?"

His voice was low, soft, and clear. Another dagger to her heart.

"No." She shook her head and swallowed hard. "It wasn't that. It wasn't even you. My friends—I let my friends embarrass me about you. Instead of finding better people to hang out with, people who might have been a better influence on me, instead of choosing to *be* a better person, I decided I didn't want to have to deal with them teasing me about you all through college. I decided it would be better if you went somewhere else. To a community college. Maybe to a trade school. Somewhere I thought guys like you belonged."

There it was. She'd said it. She'd laid the truth out there in front of him in all its ugliness.

She sniffled again and then was forced to wipe her nose on her sleeve. Somehow, she managed to keep her eyes on him until he turned to face her.

"Guys like me?"

Her tears spilled over. "Petty, huh?" she asked with a pitiful half-smile. "You weren't popular. You weren't stylish or outgoing. You were from the wrong side of town and didn't have any money. You were nowhere near as important as someone like me. What would it have looked like if I had to admit what I had done in front of everyone at school? I couldn't do that. I had a future."

"And I was nobody."

She nodded and then covered her face with both hands, letting her head drop to her drawn-up knees as she began to sob.

He was silent again, this time for a couple of minutes as he waited for her tears to subside.

"Would you like to know what happened to me after that?" he asked finally.

She forced herself to meet his gaze, knowing her eyes were puffy and bloodshot. She deserved to feel ugly in front of him. "I know you didn't go into the music program. And I know your mother—" She took a shuddering breath. "I know your mother died."

"That was in my junior year of college. But from the start, when I didn't get the scholarship, I knew I had to drop my plans for the music program and get a more practical degree." There was a touch of wryness in his expression. "I ended up in accounting. I figured it was something I could do and always have a steady job. I had a decent head for numbers, and I got a couple of grants, but money was still pretty tight. Mom was sick, had been ever since I could remember. She couldn't work the last couple of years, so I had to do what I could to keep us both going. That didn't leave me a lot of time for anything else, so you probably didn't see me around at college."

Madison blotted her face with her sleeve, wanting to say again that she was sorry, but he was probably tired of hearing that from her by now. It was a pretty pitiful response at this point anyway. It didn't erase what she'd done or make up for what she'd cost him. Not by a long shot.

"I know the trumpet meant a lot to you," she said instead.

"It did," he said. "It does."

She frowned at him, puzzled.

"I promised Mom that I'd graduate, and I did. On time and everything. I got my business degree and landed a job in a big accounting firm. I was financially stable for the first time in my life and started paying back my student loans as fast as I could. But I still had my nights and weekends. I kept playing the trumpet. I kept working, listening to the greats, trying to learn what made them great. Taking private lessons when I paid off my loans and could afford it. Do you know what I do now?"

She shook her head.

"I'm a studio musician. A producer took a chance on me and liked my work, so he talked me up to anyone who would listen. I won't bore you with the names of the artists I've backed up, but you'd recognize them. And a few of them always call me up to play for them when they have gigs out my way or when they need a sub. I never wanted to be the star, but I love the music. I love playing with guys who feel the same way, guys who get it. That I can make a living off of it is just a bonus. Some might laugh at me for saying it, but I think it's a blessing straight from God, even if I did take the scenic route to get there. So, see? You didn't ruin my life after all."

She let out her breath, relieved that he had ended up where he had, doing what he loved, but she knew none of that was thanks to her. "You must have really hated me after that day."

He shrugged. "I can't say I didn't wallow in that for a while. Maybe it was hurt more than hate, but I had to let it go. When my mom was dying, I decided I had too much to carry without adding resentment to it. Besides, who knows where I would have ended up if that hadn't happened? If nothing else, I found out who I was, what I wanted in life, and how I didn't need anyone's approval to do what I believed in. And I found out I was strong enough to keep going. So, for your part in that, thank you."

She bit her lip, determined not to cry again. "Marvin, I'm so—"

"You don't need to apologize again. I know you're sorry. And I forgive you. In fact, the main reason I came to this reunion was to let you know that face-to-face. I honestly forgive you, with no reservations. And someday, I hope you'll forgive yourself."

"Marvin—"

He gave her a little crooked smile. "And I hope you'll call me Donny. Most people do these days."

She managed a hint of a smile in return. "I'm glad. It suits you. I . . ." She sniffed again, hoping it was for the last time. "I always wanted to track you down somehow, so I could tell you how much I regretted what I did, but I was too afraid. I didn't want to face the kind of rejection I knew I deserved. But I finally got to the point where I couldn't carry it around anymore. I decided the reunion was my best chance to find you and apologize. Not only for the scholarship, but for all the years before that when I treated you like you were less than I was, when I let my friends be cruel to you and didn't stop them, when I was cruel to you myself. I hate remembering how I was. I have no excuse for it, but I know that's not who I want to be. I hope it's never me again."

"I don't think it will be. You know, even though I didn't dare to think of you as a friend back in high school, I always admired you. I always thought how nice it would be if you'd go to a dance with me or something."

He lifted one dark brow, a touch of humor in his expression. Was he actually considering . . . ? No, that would be crazy. Absolutely crazy.

"You must have gotten over that pretty fast after the scholarship thing," she said, hugging her knees again.

"Hey," he said kindly. "We're never going to get anywhere if you keep thinking like that. You asked me to forgive you and I did. That's the end of it as far as I'm concerned."

Could it be?

He stood up and held out his hand to her. "So what do you think?"

She bit her lip.

"Or are you too embarrassed to have your friends see you with Poor Marvin?"

She laughed a little as she took his hand and let him pull her to her feet. "Not if you're not too embarrassed to be seen with somebody with red eyes and grass stains on her pants."

"A little time and some cold water will get rid of the red eyes, and I bet you weren't planning on wearing those pants tonight anyway."

She clutched his hand. "Are you sure you want me to go with you?"

"Not if you're doing it because you feel sorry for me. I don't need your sympathy."

She smiled. "No, you certainly don't. In fact, I think most people would see it as a pity date, but with me being the charity case."

He tucked her arm into his and started walking back toward the inn. "We're not kids anymore. Don't we deserve a fresh chance at being friends?"

She stopped and studied his face, still unsure.

He let go of her, stepped about two feet away, and held out his hand. "Hi, I'm Marvin Donovan, but you can call me Donny. What's your name?"

That teased a grin out of her. "Madison Fields. I'm very glad to finally *really* meet you."

"There," he said, taking her arm again, "that wasn't so difficult, was it?"

She shook her head. "I can't quite believe it yet. I almost don't know how to live without that guilt behind everything I did. My whole life is a result of that one horrible decision."

"You'll learn how to let it go."

He escorted her to her room and they agreed to meet downstairs for hors d'oeuvres before going to the dance. Once he was gone, she went inside, closed the door behind her and leaned against it. Then she took a deep breath and let it out with a sigh. It was crazy, but she was going to the reunion dance with Poor Marvin. No, with Marvin Donovan. With Donny, studio trumpeter who backed big names and lived his dream. Somehow, God had turned her cruelty and selfishness into a blessing for him and she had been allowed to see it. It was time to put that time behind her for good, remembering only the lessons she had learned from it.

"Thank You," she whispered, and then she walked over to the mirror above the dresser and stared at the rumpled, stained, red-eyed girl she saw there. After a moment, she smiled.

"I forgive you."

Grace

"You don't have to go if you don't want to."

Grace checked to make sure she and Sarah were alone on the veranda. The only other one out there was Winston, and he was snoozing under one of the chairs. Madison and Donny had left for the dance only a moment before, and judging by the sparkle in Madison's eyes, Grace didn't feel like she needed to worry about her. It was as if a weight had been lifted from the younger woman, and Grace had a sneaking suspicion it had a lot to do with Donny.

Sarah, on the other hand, looked as if she were headed to the dentist's office for a root canal.

Sarah lifted her chin. "Why wouldn't I want to? It'll be fun."

"I'm sure it will be." Grace offered her a mushroom stuffed with crab and gouda. "But you don't seem particularly excited about going."

Sarah flushed slightly and waved away the hors d'oeuvre. "It's only that I don't know if this dress is going to be all right, especially after I saw Madison's. She was gorgeous."

Grace smiled slightly, wondering if that was due to Madison's lovely green dress or the change in her expression. She seemed to have shed years since just that morning.

"Anyway," Sarah said, "I wasn't planning on going to the prom when I checked in here, so I didn't bring a ball gown or anything."

"I think your dress is fine," Grace assured her, gesturing to the summery salmon-colored sheath. "Very pretty and very becoming.

But if you don't feel like going, I'm sure Keith will understand."

Sarah sighed. "It feels weird. It's not my reunion, I don't know any of the people, and I'm younger than anybody else there."

"Now, that can't be right, can it?" Grace asked. "Many of the alumni must have brought their spouses or significant others. And what's age but a number?"

"Maybe," Sarah admitted.

But you'd rather be with Aidan. Grace didn't say it aloud, but she was sure of it all the same. When she had emptied the trash can behind the front desk, she had noticed that the torn pieces of his note to Sarah weren't there anymore.

"Sometimes it's nice to spend the evening in," she said cheerfully. "I enjoy going out, but there are nights I don't want a lot of fuss."

Sarah nodded. "I'm the same way. I don't like to be rushing somewhere every night. You understand. A lot of people have to have constant entertainment, but sometimes it's nice to spend time with someone who simply wants to be with you. When I was—" She stopped herself and took a sip of her wine. "Keith is one of those who likes a lot of excitement. He always has to have something going on. One more night won't kill me."

When she was what? When she was spending time with Aidan? He seemed like the kind of guy who would enjoy doing everyday things with the woman he loved. Keith could hardly sit still for two minutes together.

"You don't exactly sound as if you think you and Keith are soul mates," Grace said lightly.

Sarah laughed. "Hardly. He's fun. I suppose that's good enough for now. It's not like I've led him on or anything. I've made sure to keep things casual between us. I may be on the rebound, but I haven't lost my mind."

"That's good to know. To some guys, 'casual' doesn't make much of a difference."

Sarah shrugged. "It's not like I'll see him again after I leave here." She glanced over toward the other side of the lake, toward The Tidewater. "And I'm sure not going to let anyone see me spending a single night of my honeymoon holed up in my suite. I don't care if he's an obnoxious jerk who's too full of himself to—Keith!"

There was a touch of defiant coquettishness in her inviting smile. He answered with a cool, appraising stare as he walked out onto the veranda.

"Nice," he said as his eyes moved from her stiletto heels to the cubic zirconia in her ears, and then he touched one finger to the matching pendant at her throat. "Very nice."

"May I get you something?" Grace asked, keeping her voice impersonal. "Tonight, we have—"

He waved her away. "Thanks, but Sarah and I really should be going." He smirked at Sarah. "I don't want us to miss the class awards. Some of us guys rigged the Biggest Beer Belly Award so Janie Corsi would win. She's about to have twins, and I want to see her face when she gets it."

"No, I suppose we can't miss something as hilarious as that." Sarah rolled her eyes as she handed Grace her wineglass. "Thanks for chatting with me, Grace. I guess I'll see you later on."

"Have a good time," Grace said, but it didn't seem likely that Sarah would enjoy the dance that much. Not when she was obviously thinking of Aidan.

"How could she not?" Keith asked, his expression smug. "She's with me."

Charlotte came out to the veranda after they left. "I guess that's everybody."

"That's all," Grace said. "Mike left early because he's on some committee or something. Madison and Donny left a few minutes ago. Together, as a matter of fact."

Charlotte grinned.

"And then you saw Keith and Sarah."

Charlotte's grin faded. "Why does she even bother with him? You can tell she's not into him at all."

"I think it's all about showing her ex-fiancé that she's having a great time without him."

"Poor guy. Maybe he's the one who's better off without her."

"I don't know about that," Grace said. "If you had seen him when he left that note—"

"You know, I never had a chance to tell you how it went with Dean today," Charlotte interrupted her.

Grace frowned, puzzled. "Dean?"

Charlotte nodded toward the door to the veranda, and Grace looked up to see Aidan standing there.

"Hello." She stood and gestured to a chair. "Come in. Would you like an hors d'oeuvre? Cheese? Wine?"

"No thank you," Aidan said. "I was only hoping I might catch Sarah here. Do you know if she's in her room?"

Charlotte immediately began clearing the table, avoiding eye contact with him and Grace.

"I'm sorry," Grace said, "but she went out a few minutes ago. Would you like to leave her a message?"

"Yeah, right," he said, "because the last one I left did so much good. I bet she tore it up and threw it in the trash without even reading it."

Grace certainly couldn't deny that, but she also knew those pieces had been fished out of the trash and taken away again. She was sure Sarah had read them, probably more than once. But she couldn't tell

Aidan any of that. It wasn't her place.

"I'm going to start cleaning up the kitchen and washing these dishes," Charlotte said, and then she smiled at Aidan. "There's still plenty of everything if you're interested."

Grace gave her a grateful nod. "I'll be there in a little bit."

Charlotte slipped inside.

Aidan put a piece of cheese on a water cracker and automatically took a bite, but it was clear he wasn't tasting the snack. Then, with a sigh, he flopped down across the table from Grace.

"Is there anything I can do to help?" she asked.

"Tell me where it all went wrong?"

He gave her a sad smile that nearly broke her heart. It would certainly be hard to deny those brown eyes anything, especially a plea to try again.

"I don't think I can help with that," she said, "but I'm a good listener if you feel like talking."

He smoothed back his thick hair. "It's not a very happy story."

She pushed the plate of cheese and crackers toward him. "The story's not over yet."

"It feels like it is." He took some cheddar and a piece of prosciutto to top off his cracker. "All but the part where I realize I misjudged her and it's time to move on."

"Are you sure about that?" Grace knew she couldn't tell him anything specific, but there had to be some way she could encourage him to not give up. "Of course, I don't know Sarah, but usually when someone's trying so hard to make people think she's having a good time, she's really not."

"Yeah, I can see she's mad."

"And hurt," Grace added softly.

"I know." He rubbed his eyes, and suddenly she realized how

deeply exhausted he must be. "And I wouldn't have hurt her for the world, but I couldn't let things go on the way they were."

"What happened?"

"I put my foot down and got both legs snapped off at the knee."

Grace winced. "Ouch."

"It's not like I expected her to agree with me, and it's not like I didn't want her to have the wedding she wanted. I only wanted her to hear me out. I wanted her to know how I felt, and she went all crazy on me. I guess I lost my temper—no, I know I did, but I thought it would all blow over and we'd work things out. That's what husbands and wives do, right? Work things out? But she wouldn't even talk to me after that. Now she's over here acting crazy with that bigmouth Keith, and I don't think I even know her anymore. What am I supposed to do?"

"You said you know this isn't like her. You know she's mad and hurt. If I were to guess, I'd say she was pretty embarrassed too. Not only about what happened with the wedding, but with how she reacted to it. It's hard to look back on things we say and do when we're upset. They're usually not pretty."

"You're right. I know I said some things I shouldn't have too. If I knew for sure that she cared about me, I wouldn't mind waiting until she cooled off. But now I'm worried she's going to do something stupid with that Keith guy just to spite me." He drew a shaky breath. "I don't know if I could stand it."

Grace had a sudden urge to hug him, as unprofessional as that would have been. She settled instead for pushing the plate of stuffed mushrooms toward him.

That seemed to amuse him, but he took one anyway.

"Now, I don't know this for sure," she said, "but I would almost bet that she did read your note."

"Why do you think that?" he asked, brightening a little.

"I know if it were me, I'd want to know what it said, even if I didn't want you to know I wanted to know."

He chuckled. "Yeah, I suppose I'd feel the same way. I guess the point now is what do I do? I've apologized. I've told her I want to talk. I've told her I still love her and that we could still have a future together if we could only get things straightened out. What's left?"

"I think you should give her a little more time to cool off." Grace couldn't tell him how reluctant Sarah had obviously felt when she was headed to the dance with Keith, but she would try to ease his mind on one point. "And I don't think you need to worry about Keith. If you're her type, he's definitely not." She couldn't keep a touch of mischief out of her expression. "But you'll never convince him of that."

"Jerk," Aidan grumbled. He ate a stuffed mushroom and his eyes widened. He grabbed another and popped it into his mouth. "These are great."

"Thank you. My sister, Charlotte, made them."

"My compliments to the chef." He watched her closely. "So you think I should leave Sarah alone for now?"

"For now. Maybe one more evening of reunion festivities at Keith's side is all it will take to bring her to her senses."

He thought that over for a minute, filling the time by eating another mushroom and then another cracker with cheddar and prosciutto. He looked a little embarrassed to see her smiling at him.

"Sorry about that," he said. "I didn't mean to eat everything."

"No, you go right ahead. Take all you want. Everyone's at the dance now anyway, so if you don't eat it, it'll go to waste."

"I never did get around to eating lunch today," he admitted. "But now that I've gotten a little of this off my chest, I'm suddenly hungry. I guess I'd better get back over to The Tidewater and get me something."

"Would you like a sandwich? We don't serve dinner in general, but that doesn't mean we couldn't whip up something for a friend."

"No," he said, standing up. "That's really nice of you, but I couldn't impose on you like that. Especially after you were so nice about listening to my sob story." He chuckled. "And *especially* after I ate all your hors d'oeuvres."

"I'm glad you're here," she said, standing too. "It won't take me more than a few minutes to put something together for you. I insist. Do you like ham?"

He nodded.

"Mustard? Swiss? Pickles?"

"Yes," he said. "All that. You got wheat bread?"

"The best ever," she assured him. "Would you like chips or apple slices?"

"Yes," he said with a grin.

"Okay, I'll be right back. Make yourself comfortable."

"Only if you'll let me pay you," he said, still standing.

"How about you eat, and we'll talk about that afterward?"

"I mean it," he said, but he sat down.

"What did he say?" Charlotte stage-whispered the moment Grace stepped into the kitchen, holding a partly scrubbed baking pan.

"He's not going to hear you from the veranda." Grace opened the refrigerator and took out what she needed to make a ham sandwich.

"For him?" Charlotte asked, going back to her scrubbing.

"He was going to go back to The Tidewater, but I convinced him he ought to eat here. On the house."

"Why am I not surprised? This is a business, and here you are giving half the inn away." Charlotte gave her a glare that wasn't nearly as stern as she'd probably meant it to be.

"One sandwich is not half the inn." Grace spread mustard on a slice of wheat bread and then arranged some sliced ham on top of it. "Besides, I'm not the only one around here who can't resist a sad story."

"I know, I know," Charlotte said piously. "Aunt Winnie is a pushover too."

"You should take a peek in the mirror," Grace advised.

Charlotte giggled. "All right, we're all pushovers, and I'm glad. So what did he say? Did he tell you what happened with him and Sarah?"

"Not much. They had a fight and now she won't talk to him. I didn't want to pry or anything."

"You didn't tell him where she was, did you?" Charlotte asked, rinsing the pan and putting it in the drying rack.

"Of course not. Only that she was out. As soon as he eats, I'm sure he'll go back to his room, and she'll never know he was here. I have a feeling that as long as he chases her, she'll keep running. From what he told me, he's said what he needs to say. He needs to let her think about it for a while and decide whether she's better off with him or without him."

Once she had finished making the sandwich and added both chips and apple slices on the side, Grace carried the plate out to the veranda, made sure Aidan had everything he needed, and then went back to the kitchen.

"Poor guy," she said, going over to the sink to dry the things Charlotte had just washed. "He's got it bad for her. If only she wasn't so stubborn about staying mad."

"Yeah," Charlotte said softly.

Grace grinned at her. "So, did you have a talk with Dean today? Or was that something you said to make Aidan think we weren't talking about him and Sarah?"

"I did, actually," Charlotte said, and then she spent several seconds scrubbing a particularly stubborn burned spot on a baking sheet.

"And?" Grace asked finally.

"And . . . I might have been wrong about a few things."

Grace raised one eyebrow.

"Okay," Charlotte said, "a lot of things. But he did steal my pork chop recipe."

"And?"

"And he admitted it and apologized and offered to take pork chops off the menu if I wanted him to."

"And you said?"

Charlotte sprayed the pan she was holding. "How could I stay mad after that? And he explained to me about a couple of things I had misunderstood or remembered wrong."

Grace couldn't quite suppress a smile. "And?"

"It's *possible* he's not such a bad guy after all." Charlotte finally looked at her, smiling too as she handed Grace the last wet pan. "And it feels good to not be carrying around all that junk I was holding against him. Not that we're best friends or anything, but we can at least be better neighbors."

"I'm so glad." Grace finished drying the pan and stowed it away with the others. "I hope Sarah will let go of some of her anger and work things out with Aidan. Even if they don't end up married, all that internal turmoil can't be good for her."

"You don't think she'll be upset if she comes back and finds him here, do you?" Charlotte asked.

"I do think she'd get over being mad if he would give her a little space, but I don't know what his being here tonight would hurt. By the time she and Keith get back, he'll be long gone."

"I wish Keith was long gone," Charlotte said, picking up a handful of dirty spoons. "I keep worrying he and Aidan are going to get into an actual brawl if they see each other again."

"I'm pretty sure he'll be out of the picture by tomorrow afternoon. Maybe by then, Sarah—" The bell above the front door jingled, and Grace sighed. "I'll get it."

She set down her dish towel and went out to reception. She stopped in her tracks to see Sarah stalking toward her.

"Sarah. You're back early. Is everything okay?"

"Where is he?" Sarah demanded.

"I thought Keith was with you."

She snorted. "He got so plastered at the dance that I didn't want to stay. I don't care. I meant where's Aidan? His car's out front. I saw it."

"I'm right here." Aidan stood in the doorway to the veranda, his empty plate in his hand. Obviously, he had heard her come in.

"Why?" Her mouth tightened into a hard line. "Why are you here?"

"I wanted to talk to you. I found out you'd gone out." He shrugged. "I stayed and ate a sandwich."

"And you couldn't get a sandwich anywhere else but here?"

"I didn't come here for the sandwich. I came here to see you."

Sarah glared at Grace. "Didn't you tell him I was out? I thought you didn't serve dinner here."

"We don't usually," Grace said as pleasantly as she was able. "But Aidan came by for the hors d'oeuvres and I found out he hadn't eaten lunch, so I offered him something a little more substantial than cheese and crackers."

Concern flashed into Sarah's eyes and then was gone. "You didn't eat?"

"I told her I'd get something at The Tidewater," Aidan said, "but she talked me into the sandwich." He gave Grace a grateful nod. "It was very good. Thank you."

Sarah scowled again. "If you've finished, you should go, shouldn't you?"

"I was hoping to talk to you."

Sarah glared at him.

"The music room is available again," Grace suggested, taking the empty plate.

"I don't have time for this," Sarah snapped.

"You'll have a lot of time without me after this," Aiden said quietly. "We're both leaving Magnolia Harbor tomorrow afternoon. I don't know if you read my note, but I wrote in there that if we didn't talk before I left, I would take that to mean you didn't see any future for us. If that's the case, I won't bother you again. If you'd actually like to talk, then now's as good a time as any, isn't it?"

Grace held her breath, afraid that if she broke the taut silence, Sarah would remember she had an audience and, for the sake of her pride, storm up the stairs to her suite. Her groomless honeymoon suite.

"All right," Sarah said, and then she noticed Grace again. "But only for a minute."

"That's all I need."

Aidan gestured toward the empty music room, and they both went inside.

"Please, Lord," Grace whispered once they shut the door after them, "lead them both the right way."

22

Sarah

The music room seemed different at night. The lights were soft, making the room feel as it might have a hundred years or more before, when it would have been bathed in candlelight and the glow of the hearth fire.

Sarah and Aidan both sat where they had the last time they talked, in the Louis XV chairs. Was it only Wednesday? It seemed forever ago. She was watching him out of the corner of her eye. Was he getting thin? Grace had said he wasn't eating. She turned her face to the dark window, not wanting him to know she was concerned. She could feel his eyes on her, but he said nothing.

"Well?" she said finally. "You were the one who wanted to talk, so talk."

"I guess now that we're here, I'm not quite sure what to say. I don't want to say the wrong thing and make things worse."

"Say whatever it is you want to say, and let's get through with it."

He shook his head. "I don't know. It seems to me like you aren't going to listen anyway. Maybe that's all I need to know."

Did she really want him to go? Forever? But if he was willing to let her go, didn't that mean he hadn't been serious in the first place? But if that was the case, why had he come here? Why had he kept trying to see her and talk to her, especially since she had done everything in the world to show him she didn't need him anymore?

She set her jaw. "You're the one who wanted out. Don't put the blame on me now."

"Sarah—"

"Don't 'Sarah' me. You don't know what it's like to be the only one in my whole family, cousins and everything, who's never been married. And I finally get engaged and plan the wedding I've always wanted and ask everybody I know to come, and then two days before we're set to get married you tell me you aren't ready? Not ready? What does that even mean? You said you loved me, and then you kicked me aside like gum on your shoe. Exactly how is that supposed to make me feel?"

He winced. "I'm sorry. I've told you that over and over again. I tried to tell you that the next day, before the wedding was called off, but you wouldn't talk to me. What was I supposed to do?"

She stared out the window again. She had refused to talk to him, even though her mother begged her to at least hear him out, even though her dad had told her about the big fight he and her mother had had only a week before their wedding, but she had been too mortified to listen. Too stunned. Too furious.

"You said it was then or never," Aidan said. "You were more concerned about what your friends might think than what I thought. I couldn't marry you under those conditions. I couldn't marry you if I wasn't sure you felt for me—for *me*—what I felt for you. What I still feel for you. I know we're different. I'm too cautious sometimes, but when I get married, I mean it to be for life. I'd rather look like a fool in front of everybody now than an even bigger fool a few years down the road after both our lives are ruined, when everyone would say, 'Well it's because they met and got married too fast.' After everything that happened those two weeks, all the wedding planning and all the showers and parties and stuff, it was too much. You know I'm not a party kind of guy. I thought you were okay with that."

"This was for our *wedding*, Aidan. I didn't expect you to live like that forever. But I've always planned out all the things I wanted to do when I got married. I've been dreaming of them for years and years. Why does it have to be about you all the time?"

A wry smile touched his mouth. "I was starting to wonder if it was about me at all."

She frowned, this time in complete confusion.

"I couldn't tell if you were more interested in having a marriage," he explained, "or just a wedding."

That stung. She would never let him see it, but it stung. She pressed her trembling lips into a tight line, knowing if she spoke, her voice would give her away. He watched her expectantly. She'd have to say something.

"All I know," she said tautly, "is that you told me you loved me and asked me to marry you. And then, out of the blue, you called the whole thing off. Why should I believe you now?"

He held out his hand—that strong, beautiful hand that had from the very start felt so right in hers. "Because I love you."

Part of her ached to run into his arms and stay there forever. Part of her—

"And," he added, "I know the way you were acting was because of the wedding, and not because that's who you really are. I guess I was surprised by it. I never pictured you as the bridezilla type."

Oh, he did not *just say that.*

"Bridezilla?" she repeated, her voice low and deceptively calm. "Did you say 'bridezilla'?"

"I didn't mean—"

"All I wanted to do was have a nice wedding. Is that a crime?"

"You're not royalty or some zillionaire celebrity or anything like that," he protested. "Why try to pretend any different?"

"You still don't understand," she said, barely keeping from sobbing.

"You don't understand it or me."

"I do understand." He exhaled heavily. "It was supposed to be your day. I didn't mind that. I wouldn't have kept you from having whatever you wanted if it made you happy. I was willing to do whatever you had planned, wear what you thought was best, say the vows however you wanted—all of it. It wasn't about any of that. It was how you treated everybody around you while you were getting everything ready. Not only me, but your friends, your brother and sister-in-law, your coworkers, even your parents, Sarah. You treated all of us as if we were just props in your personal show."

She didn't look away. She wouldn't let him see the shame that welled up inside her. But Mom had been happy to do it for her, hadn't she? She had said she was. She had said she didn't mind dealing with the florist and caterer while Sarah was having a shower at her office and another with her girlfriends and still another with her family. She had said she didn't mind hand-addressing all the invitations, even when Sarah had continued to think of more and more people to invite and insisted certain envelopes be redone because they weren't quite as pretty as the rest. And she had been so understanding when Sarah had declared at the last minute that she didn't want music played on the church organ or piano and insisted she track down a string quartet instead. And not that one that had played at Kristi Bell's wedding last year.

"Your mom did everything in the world to make this happen for you, and you ordered her around like she was your maid or something," Aidan said, his voice surprisingly gentle. He wasn't yelling at her, but the words hurt all the same. "Didn't you ever notice how tired she was?"

"I was tired, too, you know."

"Because you were out partying with your friends for two weeks straight."

"Don't be ridiculous. We did not party for two weeks straight."

"It sure felt like it." He gripped the ornate arms of the chair. "We should have been spending that time together, planning our future and anticipating our life together, but you didn't have time for me except when I was supposed to fill the traditional groom slot at the photographer's or the baker's or wherever."

"Well, excuse me for having to cram a lot into a short engagement. I wasn't about to miss something as important as—"

"You weren't about to miss out on something as important as wearing a tiara and a white T-shirt that said 'bride' on it while you and your friends stayed out all night?" He stopped himself. "Sorry. I didn't mean that to come out that way, but you should have seen yourself. It was more than just having a little fun. And your poor dad. Besides all the money he saved up for you all your life, you wanted him to go into debt for the reception because the things you had budgeted for suddenly weren't good enough? After he and your mom had worked so hard to pay off their mortgage and start putting aside something for retirement?"

"He didn't—"

She stopped herself. He didn't mind? How did she know? Had she even asked him how he felt? Had she even batted an eyelash when she found out he had cashed out some investments that were meant to provide for him and her mother later? What else had he done to pay for the wedding? She didn't know. She certainly hadn't cared. Aidan was right. She was a bridezilla.

All she wanted to do was run up to her room and bury her head under a pillow. She had been all he said and worse, last week, this week, and still he had come for her. He still loved her. How could she possibly face him now? What could she say?

"Aidan, I—"

They both jumped at the sudden pounding on the door.

"Hey, Sarah! Sarah, are you in there? Where'd you go?"

Ugh. It was Keith. Could he have worse timing?

Fuming, Sarah leapt out of her chair, marched to the door, and flung it open.

"Hey, baby," Keith said, leaning against the doorframe with what he probably considered a suave smile on his face. "Where'd you go? I looked up, and you were gone."

"I'm very sorry," Grace said, right behind him. "I tried to stop him. Please, Mr. Chastain, you really should go up to your room."

"How much have you had to drink tonight?" Sarah demanded.

"Aw, maybe two beers," Keith said.

"Yeah, in the first fifteen minutes we were there." She put her hands on her hips. "Are you crazy, driving in that condition? It's a wonder you didn't kill yourself and a lot of other people."

"Now, don't be that way, sugar. I'm not as think as you drunk I am." He giggled at his own lame joke. "Let me make it up to you. Come out on the lake with me tomorrow. I promise I'll be totally sober by then, and I won't drink anything all day. How's that?"

"I'm checking out tomorrow. There won't be time—"

"Not till three, right? Isn't that checkout time, lady?"

"That's right," Grace said, coolly professional instead of warm and inviting as Sarah was used to from her. "Would you like some help up to your room?"

"Not till I get an answer from my girl, okay? C'mon, Sarah. Just a little ride on the lake."

"Keith—" Sarah began.

"You're drunk," Aidan said, stepping between the two of them. "You need to go sleep it off."

"Aw man, are *you* back?" Keith shook his head and reached around him to grab Sarah's arm. "Come on, honey. All he ever wants to do is talk, right? We can have a lot more fun than that."

Aidan pulled his hand off of her. "I said you need to go sleep it off."

Keith's laugh was slightly louder than usual. "So that's all it takes, is it? This guy dumps you, and you're ready to run back to him the minute he snaps his fingers? I thought you women were all about empowerment and whatever else, and you let him treat you like that? Who makes your decisions? Him or you?"

Was that what she was doing, letting him decide for her? Letting him think he could get her back with a few pretty words? Did he love her or did he only want to prove he could jerk her life around anytime he wanted? Marry me, don't marry me, marry me—which was it?

"Why don't you go sit down, Sarah?" Aidan asked calmly. "I'll see he gets up to bed."

"There's a good girl," Keith added with a smirk.

"Why don't I sit down?" Sarah demanded, shaking free of Aidan. "What am I? Your dog?"

"What?" Aidan gaped at her. "How did you get that out of what I said? I'm trying to settle things down here. I'm not trying to—"

"I am perfectly able to arrange my own schedule," Sarah told him coldly while Keith smirked. "Now, if you'll excuse us, I'll settle this myself."

"Sarah, don't—"

"I said I'll settle this myself." She turned to Keith. "Now, Keith, behave yourself and go to bed and don't cause Grace any more trouble."

"But what about tomorrow?" he asked. "It's our last chance to go out on the boat."

She stared at him and then at Aidan, suddenly unsure of everything. She needed to think. She needed to be alone, get her head together, and figure out who she was and who she wanted to be. She loved Aidan, didn't she? She knew for sure she didn't even like Keith. She'd been horrible to both of them. She needed to make it right with both of them, but she couldn't do that. Not with both of them and even Grace staring at her, expecting her to make some kind of pronouncement here and now.

"Go sleep it off, okay?" She pressed both hands to the sides of her head. "Please. If you'll go now, I'll talk to you in the morning, all right? But only if you're not drinking."

"Promise?" Keith asked, perking up.

"Yeah, all right. Now go."

"Hey, sorry man," Keith told Aidan with exaggerated concern. "Hope I didn't interrupt." With a little wave, he walked out of the room and weaved toward the stairs.

"Sarah," Aidan began as soon as Keith was out of sight, but she shook her head. She had already snapped at him for nothing. She didn't want to risk doing that again.

"Can we talk about this tomorrow too? I have to think. About everything."

She couldn't sort through it all standing here in front of him. Aidan had shown her herself, and the sight hadn't been a pretty one. There had to be a way she could take a step back from the person she had been for the past several weeks and be herself again, the girl Aidan had fallen in love with.

"Please," she said, knowing if she had to say much more than that, she'd make a bigger fool of herself than she had already.

Aidan only nodded.

Before she started crying right there, she turned and ran up to her room.

Grace

"I'm sorry," Grace said quietly when she and Aidan were alone. "I tried to stop him, but he was already banging on the door before I could."

"It's all right."

He really did have a charming smile, even if it was a little bittersweet right now. She couldn't imagine how Sarah could resist it or why she had agreed to see Keith again, but it was obvious to Grace that the younger woman had felt conflicted and confused and ashamed.

"You know," Grace said, "I think she was right. She needs some time to think. Whatever you two talked about definitely upset her, and Keith only made it worse."

"I made it worse," Aidan said. "I made sure to tell her everything she did wrong and how thoughtless she'd been and who all she had hurt. No wonder she doesn't want to be around me anymore."

"I don't know about that. From what I could see, she was embarrassed. I think she needed that talk. She's probably just trying to figure out what to do now."

"Do you think so?" he asked, hope igniting in his eyes.

"I don't know her well enough to be sure of anything, but I also didn't notice anything that made me think now was the time to give up hope."

"But that Keith guy—"

"That's something else I didn't see any sign of," Grace said, unable to keep from smiling.

"What?"

"Her being interested in him. I'm not sure why she agreed to see him tomorrow, but I don't think it's because she's planning on seeing him again. Give her a little space and see what happens."

He nodded. "I should have done that in the first place instead of chasing after her like I've been doing."

"At least she knows you care about her. If nothing else, she can't say you didn't try."

"Yeah." He shoved his hands into his pockets. "Too little, too late."

She patted his shoulder. "Not yet. I think the best thing you could do is go back to your room and get a good night's sleep. Give her time to think. Be there when she needs you."

"I can do that. Thanks." He reached into his pocket. "How much do I owe you?"

"Nothing. The sandwich is on the house."

"Can't do it," he said, pressing a few bills into her hand. "I can't have you and your sister go bankrupt because of me."

"If a sandwich breaks us, we shouldn't be in the business anyway."

But he refused to take the money back. "Someday, if things work out, I'll come back here with Sarah and you can treat us both like royalty."

"It would be our pleasure."

"Thanks for the support," he said, and then he smiled. "And for the sandwich and everything else." He stepped outside and then turned back one final time. "Oh, and tell your sister she's a great cook. Those crab things were so good. She ought to have her own cooking show or at least publish her recipes."

"She doesn't have a show," Grace told him, "but she does have books. Look up Charlotte Wylde sometime."

"I'll do that. And you should have a show too."

"Me?" She laughed. "I'm not a gourmet cook."

"Maybe not, but you give good advice. Thank you."

"What happened?" Charlotte asked once Grace went back into the kitchen. "What happened? It didn't come to blows, did it?"

"Of course not." Grace poured herself a cup of coffee and sat at the table. "Though I wasn't too sure that wouldn't happen after Keith started pounding on the music room door. You never know what people will do when they're drunk."

"I was ready to call the police if he didn't settle down in a hurry."

"He's probably passed out on his bed by now." Grace shook her head. "At least he'll be checking out tomorrow. Hopefully his buddy Mike will check on him when he gets back from the dance."

"From what I can tell, this isn't the first time Keith's been in that condition. Mike's probably been watching out for him since their college days."

The bell over the front door rang, and Grace got to her feet. "That might be him now."

She could hear the murmur of voices when she got to the kitchen door, and she paused for a moment. That wasn't Mike. It was a man's voice, yes, but it was deeper and richer than Mike's. She heard a woman's soft laugh, a moment or two of silence, and then the two of them exchanged good nights.

Charlotte gave her a puzzled frown.

"I think it's Madison and Donny. Sounds like he's gone upstairs."

"I wonder how the dance was."

"I couldn't hear what they were saying," Grace admitted, "but from the tone of their voices, I'd say they both had a good time."

She pushed open the kitchen door a crack and saw Madison standing at the end of the front desk writing something on the inn stationery that was always available there.

"Did you have fun at the dance?" Grace asked, joining her.

Madison pulled the half-filled paper a little closer to herself and covered most of it with one hand, but she smiled. "It was fun," she said, and then she giggled. "Donny won the award for Most Changed."

Grace smiled. "He wouldn't be the first late bloomer in the world, but he's certainly a very attractive man now. I bet he surprised a lot of people."

"I think he did, and so did I. My friends couldn't believe he was the same guy we went to school with or that I had come to the dance with him."

"School days don't last forever," Grace said.

Madison exhaled heavily. "Thank goodness." She glanced at the page she had been writing on and then inquiringly at Grace.

"I guess I'd better get back to the kitchen," Grace said. "Is there anything you need?"

"No, thank you. All I need is a good night's sleep, and I plan to get started on that as soon as I finish this."

Grace nodded. "Good. Sleep well."

She went back into the kitchen, where she and Charlotte finished tidying up for the night. Once Charlotte had gone back to her cottage, Grace went out to the front desk. The lobby was empty, and the notepad Madison had been writing on was blank. Either she had taken the page she had written on with her or . . .

With a quick look around to make sure she was alone, Grace went to the hatbox and opened it. There on top of the other notes was a piece of inn stationery, folded in half. On the outside, in a striking feminine hand, was written, *If you need forgiveness . . .*

Unable to resist, Grace opened the note.

If you need forgiveness, it's never too late, as long as you're willing to ask for it.

Grace read the whole thing. In a few words, it told the story of a girl who had been cruel and thoughtless and the boy she had hurt. It also told the story of the woman who had come searching for forgiveness and who had finally found it and, more than that, peace.

Maybe there's more to the story of the girl and the boy. Maybe there's not. I don't know yet. But I know I don't have to carry around my guilt anymore. I know I'm not that girl anymore, thank God. But I pray that someone else will read this and find the courage to ask for forgiveness too. It's worth it.

Grace felt more than a little tightness in her throat as she refolded the note and put it back into the hatbox. She hoped so too.

Sarah

"Don't let him give up on me," Sarah prayed for what must have been the hundredth time that night. "Please, God. Help me make everything right with everybody."

There were so many people she needed to apologize to. She rolled over again, unable to find a comfortable position even though the bed itself was the epitome of luxury. She had to straighten things out once and for all.

She'd start with the easiest wrong to right. She had to apologize to Keith for the way she had used him, and she would make it clear that her future was with Aidan. "If Aidan will still have me," she muttered.

Still, she would feel better about everything once Keith was taken care of. She knew he didn't actually care about her. Surely, when he was sober, he'd shrug off any apology and say it had all been in fun, but she had to apologize anyway. It was the right thing to do.

If only Aidan would understand too.

She turned over again. Things hadn't ended very well last night. He couldn't have a clue how she was feeling or how much she wanted to try again with him. But she'd see to that too. Just as soon as she'd dealt with Keith.

How nice it would be to spend a quiet afternoon with Aidan, the two of them rummaging through antique stores or exploring the woods around the lake. This was supposed to be her honeymoon week, and she had spent it rushing through events she didn't care about with someone she didn't even like. She stuffed her head under the pillow, trying hard not to start crying again. This was how Aidan must have felt the week before their wedding. She was such an idiot.

But he had still come for her. He had still tried to make her see what she had been doing. He had still loved her and wanted her. She wasn't going to throw that away anymore. She wasn't going to throw it away ever again.

The next morning, Sarah sat out on the veranda eating eggs Benedict and waiting for Keith to come downstairs. If she was lucky, he wouldn't even remember what she'd said last night about the boat and she could apologize to him right there at breakfast and get it over with. But knowing Keith, he'd probably insist they go out on the boat to talk. She probably owed him that much after the way she had used him. She had brought her big floppy sun hat and that charming hatpin Grace's aunt had given her to keep the wind from blowing it away. At least she wouldn't get sunburned.

Just as she was hoping Keith would be too hungover to come down for breakfast, he showed up. His face was a little puffy and pale, but his usual smarmy grin was firmly in place. Mike was right behind him, looking faintly annoyed.

"Hey there," Keith said, slipping into the chair next to her. "Are you about ready to go sailing with me?"

"Wouldn't you like breakfast?" she asked, but his face paled at her words.

"I'd rather get a little fresh air first."

"I thought we could talk here, you know? We both have a lot to do before we check out, and—"

"Aw, come on. Don't be like that, not on our last day."

"I told you that you ought to forget about that stupid boat," Mike grumbled, helping himself to bacon.

"See?" Keith pressed. "This is why we need some privacy for our talk. You do want to talk, don't you?"

She did, but certainly not in his room or her own. The music room? No, her talk with Aiden was too fresh in her mind. She needed to deal with one apology at a time.

"Yes, okay," she said. "If you're sure you don't want anything to eat. I'm nearly through."

Mike snickered. "Don't get seasick out there, man."

Keith sneered at him as he stood up, but then he blanched and quickly sat back down.

"Are you sure this is a good idea?" Sarah asked him.

"Just stood up too fast, that's all." He took a couple of deep breaths and then nodded. "Maybe I'll have a cup of coffee."

Mike poured him one. "Remember we have to be out by three."

Keith hunched over his coffee cup. "Yeah, sure. Whatever."

Sarah smiled at Mike. "You sound like you're eager to get back home."

"I miss the family, you know? Don't get me wrong, this week was fun. Mostly. But I'm ready to go back to who I am now."

Sarah nodded. She was ready to go back too. To her friends. To her family. To Aidan. To herself.

She drank the last of her orange juice and stood up. "Ready?"

Keith got up and put on his sunglasses. "You're gonna miss me when I'm gone."

Mike rolled his eyes. "Come on, man. You don't really think—"

"We've got a couple of things to talk about," Sarah said, not wanting to say anything to Keith in front of him. "Excuse us."

With a touch of swagger, Keith got up, took her arm, and led her out to the dock.

25

Grace

The oven timer dinged, and Grace hurried to take out the pan of cinnamon rolls she had made. It was Charlotte's turn to go to church that week, but the two of them always spent part of Saturday night planning a good breakfast menu that one of them could handle alone the next morning. Grace always missed the wisdom of Pastor Glen's sermons and the wonderful worship the church members shared when it was her turn to watch the inn, but it was still a glorious Sunday morning, and the view of the lake from the veranda looked like a preview of Heaven.

She set the pan on top of the stove to let it cool and cut up some fresh fruit to set out with it. It was probably too soon to make more coffee, but perhaps Keith would need an extra cup or two to get him going again after last night. She'd check when she went back out to the veranda.

She was surprised to find Mike out there alone. "Hasn't your friend come down yet?"

"He went out on the lake with Sarah." Mike shook his head. "I keep trying to tell him that she's not interested in him, but I guess that only makes him more determined."

Grace's concern must have shown on her face.

"Oh, don't worry," Mike said. "He wouldn't hurt her or anything. He just likes to dump somebody before she can dump him."

Grace shook her head, deciding it was wiser to keep her mouth shut. Keith and Sarah would both be leaving this afternoon, and that would be the end of it. She went back into the kitchen to check the pantry and the cleaning supplies for anything they might be running low on, and before she knew it, Charlotte was home from church.

"I brought you a surprise," she said, stepping aside to reveal Winnie standing behind her.

"A delightful surprise." Grace hurried over to hug her aunt and invited her to sit down. "How was church?"

"A good, practical sermon," Winnie said. "All about meeting people's needs right where they are."

Grace gave her a rueful smile. "If they'll let you." She told them briefly about Sarah going rowing on the lake with Keith. "I can't see any good coming from her going out there with him."

"We don't know all the facts," Charlotte said. "And people have to work things out their own way."

"You can't push them." Winnie patted Grace's arm. "But you know that already. I think you do more good than you realize by listening when people want to talk and offering good advice. Besides, we don't always see the results when we help someone. That's God's business. All we need to do is keep helping when we can right where we are." She winked at Charlotte. "End of sermon. I thought you'd like a recap since you couldn't be there."

"I just wish—" Interrupted by the front doorbell, Grace sighed and got up. "Be right back." She pushed open the kitchen door and then turned back to Charlotte and Winnie. "It's Aidan. What do I tell him?"

"Why don't you go see what he wants, and then you'll know?" Winnie suggested. "I'll go with you."

They went into the lobby together.

Aidan had dark bags under his eyes, and his face was pale. He obviously hadn't slept well, if at all. "Listen, I know I was supposed to give

Sarah a little space, but the way she left things last night, especially with that Keith guy—I really need to talk to her. Do you know where she is?"

"Well," Grace began.

"She's out on the lake with Keith," Winnie said brightly. "But I don't know when they'll be back."

Grace looked at her, startled, and Aidan clenched his jaw.

"I guess that's it," he said. "No use sticking around anymore."

"Please wait until you can talk to her," Grace said quickly. "I don't know why she went, but she didn't look like she actually wanted to. My guess is she wanted to let him know she's not interested in him."

"She could have just told him," Aidan muttered.

"They ought to be coming back soon," Grace said. "Why don't you wait and ask her about it then?"

"Or," Winnie said with a glint in her eye, "you could go out and see what's going on. There's a little rowboat down at the dock. It belongs to the inn, but I'm sure my nieces won't mind you using it."

"Aunt Winnie," Grace said sternly, "perhaps he'd be better off waiting for them here."

"And perhaps Sarah needs rescuing," Winnie replied. "You never know what men like that might be up to."

Aidan's hands clenched into fists. "You don't think he'd try something, do you?"

Winnie shook her head. "You never know."

"Is it all right if I use that boat?" he asked Grace.

"Sure." She glanced at her aunt. "Help yourself."

He bolted out through the veranda door and was gone.

"Why in the world did you tell him that?" Grace asked Winnie once he was gone. "I'm sure Sarah can take care of herself."

Winnie shrugged. "I only knew he ought to borrow the boat. Not to worry."

"And then what?"

"Good heavens, honey, I have no idea. That's none of my business." She took Grace's arm and sauntered toward the kitchen with her. "Now, Charlotte and I were talking about fixing up something special for lunch. I just happened to remember a recipe for chicken-fried steak your great-grandma used to make when I was a girl, and I think we should try it."

"You know," Grace said, giving her a huge hug, "I think you're right."

26

Sarah

A gust of wind tugged at Sarah's hat, and she reached up to make sure it was secure. The hatpin was still firmly in place, so she put her hands back into her lap and watched Keith lazily rowing toward the middle of the lake.

"Isn't this far enough?" she asked. "This is as good a place to talk as any."

"C'mon, babe," he said. "You don't have to make excuses to be with me."

She wanted to roll her eyes, but that probably wouldn't be the most mature way to start a conversation about apologizing for making immature choices. "I'm sorry for the way I've treated you, Keith. I wanted to let you know that. I have no excuse for it."

"I knew you'd eventually come around." Somehow, he managed to look even more smug than usual. "You resisted longer than most girls."

"Keith! I don't mean that at all. I mean—"

"Oh, I get it. You're still mad because I got wasted last night at the dance. Come on now. Everybody had a few."

"I don't know how many you had," she told him sternly, "but it was more a few."

"You're not going to hold that against me, are you? All I wanted was to have a little fun with the guys." He let the oars slide down into the oarlocks on either side of the boat and leaned toward her. "Besides, it's only you and me here now. Nobody to get in the way."

He put one hand on her bare knee, and she immediately pushed it off.

"I think it's time to go in now."

He gave her a snide little grin. "I thought we were just getting started." He grabbed her hands. "You've been after me all week. This is your last chance."

She jerked her hands away. "I thought you would have sobered up since last night, but if you're not plastered, I don't know how you could imagine that."

His smile turned hard, and he picked up the oars again and started rowing. He wasn't rowing toward the shore.

"What are you doing?" she asked. "I want to go in."

"Relax, baby," he said, not even slowing down. "I'm just going to find us a more secluded spot."

"Are you out of your mind? Do you think you're still in college with your frat-boy friends? Give me those."

She tried to grab the oars, but he only shoved her away and rowed harder.

"Play nice," he panted. "It's a long swim back to shore."

She glanced to her right. It might take her a few minutes to reach land, but it wasn't an unreasonable prospect. She hadn't done much swimming in the past few years, but she was sure she could manage it.

Suddenly she remembered his aversion to water.

"Fine," she said. With a cold smile, she pulled the long, sharp pin out of her hat. "At least I won't be making the swim alone."

"No, no, wait!"

She jabbed the pin into the right side of the boat, and the air started rushing out.

"Great." He huffed and kept rowing. "Not that that's going to make any difference. These boats have a lot of little compartments sealed off from each other, so if one leaks, the others will keep the boat afloat."

"How many others?" she asked innocently, and she plunged the pin into the left side of the boat.

"Devil," he spat, rowing faster.

She merely smiled and punctured the bottom of the boat. With a curse, he dropped the oars into the oarlocks and tried to wrench the pin out of her grasp. She managed to turn it enough to draw blood down the length of his arm. He sucked in a breath, cradling his arm against his chest.

She calmly punctured the boat in several more places. It was taking on water now. Fast.

He grabbed the oars again, face blanched and knuckles white, and tried to row again. But it was too late. "Are you crazy?"

They were more than ankle deep now, the water rushing in faster and faster.

She slipped off her sandals, surprising herself with her own calm. "I guess you'd better start swimming, Mr. White-water Man."

He was rowing frantically now, useless as it was. "Don't you understand, you lunatic? I can't swim. I can't swim!"

Fabulous. She wasn't afraid of swimming to shore herself. It couldn't be more than a couple of hundred yards. But what would she do with 170 pounds of flailing, terrified blowhard?

She looked behind her. Someone was paddling a rowboat toward them at a pretty good clip, but the glint of the sun off the lake water made it hard to see who it was.

Keith began waving his arms, and Sarah winced at the red streak down one of them. She didn't think he'd need stitches or anything, but still.

"Over here!" Keith howled. "Over here!"

In another minute or two, their boat would be little more than a soggy wad of heavy plastic, and they'd be neck deep in Lake Haven. She stuck her hatpin back into her hat, hoping she wouldn't lose it if she had to swim, and then peered at the rowboat again. Was it—? Was it Aidan? The boat came closer so that she could see how the man moved, and she was sure that it must be.

"Are you okay?" he called as he pulled up next to them. "Better put these on, both of you."

Aidan tossed out a life jacket, and Keith grabbed it and struggled into it. His expression faintly disgusted but unsurprised, Aidan held on to the second, opting to hold out his hand to Sarah instead. "Better get in and then put it on. Otherwise he might decide he needs two."

With a grateful smile, she took his hand and stepped into his boat. Her movement was enough to overwhelm the inflatable, and Keith went down, arms flailing as he bobbed in the water. "I can't swim! I can't swim!"

"Hence the life jacket," Aidan said, tossing him a line. "You're not going anywhere."

Keith grabbed the rope and hauled himself over to the boat, but Aidan stopped him when he tried to pull himself over the side.

"Sorry, man, but there's only room for two."

"But she can swim," Keith gasped, his face crumpling as if he might burst into tears.

"So can I," Aidan assured him, only the tiniest hint of a grin at the corner of his mouth. "But you'd better hang on."

Sarah could have kissed him right then and there.

It didn't take long for Aidan to row them back to the dock at the inn. He helped Sarah out of the boat first and then hauled Keith out of the water after her.

"Next time make sure you and your passenger have life jackets, especially if you don't know how to swim," Aidan told Keith. "Not drowning is a lot more important than looking cool. Got it?"

Keith glared at him, lake water puddling around his feet, and then he nodded toward Sarah. "From what I've seen, if you take that one back, you're going to wish you'd let her drown."

Sarah wanted to remind him that she hadn't been the one in danger of drowning, but then she remembered that she had used him to make Aidan jealous, that she had never been interested in him as a person. To her, he had only been a tool, a way she made herself feel wanted. What a mess she was.

She winced slightly. "Keith, I'm sorry. I guess I've been too wrapped up in my own situation to be a very nice person. I started out wanting to have a little bit of fun and to forget why I came here in the first place. Then, when Aidan showed up, I knew it bugged him that I was going out with you, so I kept doing it." She glanced at Aidan. "I haven't been very good about considering anyone else's feelings lately. I'm sorry. I really am."

"Forget about it," Keith snapped. "It's not like I had anything permanent in mind. I was going to dump you anyway." He gave her a once-over and sneered at Aidan. "Good luck, man. You're going to need it."

With that, he strode up the path to the inn, his shoes squishing with every step.

"Are you all right?" Aidan asked when he was out of earshot.

Sarah nodded. "I know he didn't care anything about me. He was only trying to impress his friends, but I should never have treated him the way I did." She gazed up into his eyes. "Or you."

"I guess we both messed up." He took her hands in his, pulling her a little closer. "I never should have asked to call off the wedding in the first place. I regretted it the minute I did it. If I hadn't let my temper get the best of me that night, we would have been here together all week instead of in separate hotels. What kind of a ridiculous arrangement is that?"

She tried to laugh, but her throat was suddenly tight. "You were right about me. I was so mad about not getting what I wanted, I didn't care what kind of collateral damage I left in my wake." She ducked her head, knowing her face was flushed with shame. "I guess the only thing worse than a bridezilla is a bridezilla throwing a temper tantrum."

"I shouldn't have called you that," he murmured.

"You said it because it was true. You were right about how I treated people. My friends. My family. I didn't even see it." She gave him a pitiful little smile. "I probably will have been disowned by all of them by the time I get home. I don't know why any of them put up with me."

"Because they wanted you to have the wedding day you always dreamed of," he said. "Because they love you."

She knew that, and the knowledge just made everything worse. They were the people she should have been good to, not the ones she should have used and taken for granted. A sudden thought struck her.

"How did you manage to pay Dad back?" she asked. "You said you sent him a check for the cost of the reception."

"So, you did read my note."

She nodded.

"I borrowed against that property my grandmother left me," he said. "Only temporarily. Once I find a buyer, for part of it at least, then I'll pay off the loan." He shrugged a little. "I was the one who called everything off. I didn't want your parents to have to take the hit for it."

Her parents. She would have a lot of apologies to make when she got back home. She had a pretty important one to make right now.

"I didn't mean to be that crazy," she said, her voice pitifully thin. "I guess I expected everybody to be as excited about the wedding as I was."

"I was just excited about you," he told her. "I would have been as happy to run off to the justice of the peace and then put all that money into a house on the property I had. Something we could enjoy for more than one evening."

He had mentioned that idea once before, right after they'd gotten engaged, but she had swept the suggestion aside with a dismissive laugh. The memory made her cringe.

"I'm so sorry," she choked out, looking up at him again, seeing the pain and uncertainty in his eyes. "After everything I said and did back home, you still came here to try to work things out. After the way I treated you here, you still came out on the lake to help me."

"No matter what you decide about me, about us, I wasn't about to let that jerk push you around. Grace's aunt said there was a rowboat I could use if I wanted to. I had planned to wait on the dock until you two came back in, but then I saw you fighting with him, and I figured you could use a ride."

"You should have left me to swim back. I deserved at least that."

"Why would I want that?" He leaned a little closer to her and pushed her hair behind her ear. "I love you."

The words hung there in the air waiting for her to either clutch them to her heart or swat them to the ground.

"Still?"

The word was only a pathetic squeak, but he pulled her to him, his lips barely a whisper away from hers.

"Always."

His kiss sent a surge of warmth from her lips all the way down to her wet feet.

She melted against him. "I don't care about the wedding. I don't care about the money. I just want to know if it's too late." She twined her arms around his neck and pulled him close to rest her forehead against his. "Is it too late for us?"

"Not unless you say it is." He touched his lips to hers again. "I love you."

He offered those precious words again, and this time she didn't hesitate to grab them. "I love you too," she murmured. "As much as I tried to convince myself otherwise, I never stopped."

She stood tiptoe to kiss him again, clinging to him so her knees wouldn't buckle.

He lifted her off the ground anyway and spun her around with a laugh. "Does this mean we're on again?"

She nodded rapidly, coherent speech escaping her.

He hugged her tight, then set her on her own feet again. "Do you want to wait a while to get married, or—"

"I wish the JP's office was open on Sundays."

That made him laugh. "But they're open on Mondays. We already have the license and everything."

"At home," she huffed.

"Actually, they're over at The Tidewater."

"You mean—" She licked her suddenly dry lips. "You mean Monday? As in tomorrow Monday?"

"Tomorrow Monday is exactly the Monday I had in mind. What do you say?"

She could only gape at him.

"I guess your friends and family will think we're crazy if we come back married," he said. "Will you mind?"

"I think they'll all be glad there won't be another wedding to plan for." She kissed him again. "Besides, by then, I'll be too happy to care."

With their arms around each other's waists, they returned to the inn. Grace was tidying up the front desk while Charlotte freshened the spray of roses on one of the end tables. Sarah's face turned warm when she saw the glance the sisters exchanged as she and Aidan came in together.

"You found her," Grace said with a warm smile.

"I did." Aidan squeezed Sarah a little bit closer to his side. "At last."

Sarah put her hand up to smooth her hair and touched instead the hat she had forgotten was still there—thanks to the hatpin.

"Do me a favor," she told Grace. "Tell your aunt the hatpin came in handy after all."

"She left a few minutes ago to get an old recipe from her house. She ought to be back soon, and then you can tell her yourself."

"I think we'd both like to thank her," Aidan said.

"After Keith came in and stormed up the stairs, I was afraid you might have ended up in the water too, Sarah. I'm glad you didn't." Charlotte gave her sister a sly glance. "At any rate, I think he'll have plenty of time to get changed and packed in time for checkout."

"Checkout." Sarah gasped. "What time is it? I guess I have to get packed."

"No rush," Grace assured her. "Checkout's at three, but we won't charge you for another day if you take a little longer. We don't have a reservation for your suite until a week from now. Take your time."

Aidan squeezed Sarah's shoulders again, sending another frisson of warmth through her.

"So, anybody can reserve that suite for the coming week?" he asked Grace.

"Anybody," she said. "Do you know anyone who's interested?"

"What do you think, Sarah?" Aidan asked. "A trip to the JP first thing tomorrow and then another week here? Together this time?"

If she made a sound, she knew the tears would start running down her face. She buried her face in his shoulder and nodded.

He pressed a kiss into her hair. "That okay with you, Grace?"

"I'll extend your reservation for the Dogwood Suite through next Sunday. How's that?"

"That would be great." He tilted Sarah's face up to him. "So, what do you think? Dinner tonight? And maybe before that we could spend some time at that antique place I saw driving up here?"

She beamed at him. "Really? That was one of the places I had hoped we could check out while we were here."

"You got it. Want to go now?"

She giggled. "I don't even have shoes on." She grinned at Grace and Charlotte. "He never cares how I look."

"Sure I do," he said. "You look happy. What else could I want?"

How had she ever done without him all this time? How could she have risked losing him?

"Give me a minute," she said, touching her lips to his cheek. "I'll be right back down."

"I'll be waiting."

She hurried up to her room, refreshed her makeup, ran a comb through her tousled hair, and grabbed a pair of shoes. She didn't know why she needed them, though. She was sure her feet weren't going to touch the ground for the rest of the day.

Charlotte

"I wish I'd been a fly on the wall when Sarah and Keith were out in that boat," Charlotte said when Sarah and Aidan had left. "Or a dragonfly on the lake."

"I don't know exactly what happened, but Keith didn't come back with his inflatable boat." Grace laughed softly. "I'm guessing Aunt Winnie's hatpin had something to do with that."

Charlotte glanced toward the front door. "I'm so glad those two worked things out. Even as recently as this morning, I would never have thought they'd get back together."

"I'm glad you and Dean worked things out too."

Charlotte shrugged. "Not quite the same situation, but yeah, I'm glad too. It's nice to know I was wrong about him. And, to tell the truth, it's nice to not be mad at him anymore. I didn't realize how much resentment I was carrying around all the time until I let it go. But I still want to have a little talk with Laurie."

"Just don't let her get to you," Grace said.

The phone rang, and Charlotte picked it up and read the caller ID. "Hi, Dean."

"Hey," Dean said. "Listen, I told you I'd let you know next time Laurie showed up."

"Laurie?" Charlotte asked. That was a coincidence.

"Yeah, she's here now."

"She is?" Charlotte raised her eyebrows at Grace.

"I told her I'd buy her a cup of coffee," Dean said, "so I'm sure she'll be here for a few minutes anyway. Can you come by?"

"Hang on." Charlotte put one hand over the phone. "Mind if I run over to Dean's? Laurie's there, and I'd like to put an end to this rumor business once and for all."

"Sure," Grace said. "Go."

"I'll be back in plenty of time to make the hors d'oeuvres." Charlotte put the phone back up to her ear. "Dean, I'll be right there. Don't let her get away."

"Don't worry," Dean said, and there was a chuckle in his voice. "We'll be here when you get here."

Charlotte peered into the dining room at The Tidewater, expecting to find Dean and Laurie drinking coffee and having ever so good a time, but the dining room was empty except for someone putting fresh cloths on all the tables.

She turned to go into the main lobby, where she found the same young woman at the reception desk as on her last visit.

"Mr. Bradley is waiting for you in his office," she said before Charlotte could say anything.

"Thanks."

Charlotte went around to the office door and knocked.

Dean answered immediately. "Charlotte. Come in. Laurie and I were having a cup of coffee. Would you like something?"

"Coffee would be great." Charlotte sat in the empty chair next to Laurie. "Hello there. How are things at the Omni these days?"

"Oh, fine," Laurie said airily, but it was obvious she hadn't expected anyone to interrupt her little tête-à-tête with Dean—especially not Charlotte. She sat up a little straighter, holding her cup and saucer in both hands and turning her knees slightly to one side, clearly showing off the strappy sandals that accentuated her slender calves and ankles. Her bright-white sundress set off her golden tan and flaming hair, and judging by her posture, she was well aware of it.

Charlotte didn't say anything else for a moment. She hoped Dean would be the one to bring up the gossip about her recipes. She sipped her coffee which, like everything else at The Tidewater, was excellent. Perhaps it would be a good opener.

"This is very good," she said at last, holding up her coffee cup. "Have you ever considered offering specialty coffees and things like that here, Dean? I had a wonderful vanilla latte at the Dragonfly yesterday. The espresso was good, too, wasn't it, Laurie?"

"Delicious," Laurie said, a sudden tautness in her voice as she set down her cup and fumbled for the little beaded bag at her feet. "I'd better get going. I only stopped by to say hello, and I see you two have business to discuss."

"Don't go," Dean said mildly.

"Please," Charlotte added. "We ought to talk."

"Another time," Laurie said. "I really need to—"

"You really need to listen," Dean said. "Just for a few minutes, I promise."

"I have to get back to the Omni. I'm supposed to meet with some of the new vendors about our seafood, and I'd hate to keep them waiting."

He looked unimpressed. "You told me that wasn't until tomorrow. It's Sunday, remember?"

"Of course," she said with a nervous giggle. "Don't be silly. I meant I have to get things ready for the meeting. The manager at the restaurant practically begged me to take over for him with that, and

I've been researching wholesale prices and availability and everything else so I'll know if they're offering a good deal. I don't want to mess this up, you know?"

"I thought you were the hostess," he said.

"That's my technical job description, but I practically manage the place. I have a feeling that when he moves up, he'll want me to take his place."

"Is that true?" Dean peered at her. "Or is it only something you hope happens someday?"

"Well, that's not very nice. I think I'd know more about my job than you, wouldn't I?"

Dean nodded gravely. "And I think I'd know more about what I said and what I didn't say than you."

She glared at Charlotte. "What has she been telling you, Dean? You know she's just jealous."

"Of what?" he asked.

"Of—of—" She huffed. "Oh, it doesn't matter. Think what you want. I have better things to do than stand here and be accused of things that aren't true."

"Maybe I misunderstood what you said back at the coffee shop," Charlotte ventured. "I thought you said Dean was the one who was claiming my signature recipes weren't original."

Laurie sat there biting her lip and twisting her fingers together. "I thought he was. You know how mad he's been at you since we all worked back at the Crab. He won't admit it, I know, but it's true."

"Actually," Dean said, "it's not. I'm not saying we didn't have our disagreements, and I'm not saying I didn't do and say some stupid things, but if I've been mad at anybody all this time, it's been at myself for not handling things better than I did. And to make it very, very clear, I never at any time told anyone that Charlotte's recipes weren't her creations. Do you understand, Laurie?"

Laurie sniffed.

"And," Dean added, "I'd appreciate it if you wouldn't go around telling people things about me that aren't true. Like that we're dating."

"I never said we were dating," she spat, glaring at Charlotte once more. "Just that we saw each other off and on, which is true."

Charlotte shot Dean a sideways glance, and he gave her a subtle nod, indicating that he believed her version of the story.

"I'm sorry, Laurie," Charlotte said. "I don't want to hurt your feelings or embarrass you, but in this business, reputation is very important. And in or out of business, my reputation is important to me. I'd rather let this rumor about my recipes fade away and never say another word about it. If you'll let that happen, then I won't have to tell people the truth of the matter the next time the subject comes up. Won't that be the easiest way for both of us to handle it?"

Laurie was standing now, clutching her bag in both hands, huffing like a bull about to charge.

"Do you agree?" Charlotte asked finally.

"Fine," Laurie snapped, and she stalked to the door and opened it. "I won't say another word about your stupid recipes, but I will say I hope you two are happy together. You deserve each other."

With that, she stormed out of the office, giving the door a rattling slam behind her.

"Okay then," Charlotte said once the tsunami had passed.

Dean shook his head. "I guess that could have been worse. I don't know how, but I'm sure it's possible."

"I'm glad it's over. I don't know what that was at the end, about us deserving each other."

He shrugged. "I guess the only way she could explain my not wanting to go out with her was that I was interested in you."

"Some people can't believe a man and a woman can just be friends," she said, hoping her embarrassment didn't show.

"I don't know why not. And, when it comes down to it, I hope the woman I marry is my best friend first."

He could be so sweet when he wanted to be.

"I think that's a wonderful basis for a marriage. Did you tell that to the matchmaker?"

He laughed. "Not in so many words, no, but it doesn't matter. I told you I'm not going back there."

"Why not? You don't have to worry about being matched with me again. I've already withdrawn from the service."

"So have I," he said. "After all this, I think I'll take a break for a while. I've always heard that the best way to find the right one is to stop looking and simply live your life."

"Good advice. I think I'll do that myself." She stood up and handed him her cup.

"Leaving?" he asked, standing too.

"Grace and I are going to have lunch with Aunt Winnie. Her grandmother's famous chicken-fried steak. Besides that, nearly everybody staying with us will be checking out soon, and I promised Grace I'd be back in time to do the hors d'oeuvres too. You know how it is, trying to keep a place running smoothly."

"Sounds like you have a busy afternoon ahead," he said with an enigmatic smile. "But can you wait just one more minute? I want to show you something."

"Okay."

"One minute." He loped out of the room and was back less than a minute later, one of the Tidewater's dinner menus in his hand.

She shook her head. "Oh, Dean, you didn't actually change your menu because of the pork chops, did you? I told you that you didn't have to. Really, it's not a big deal."

"Now, now," he said, putting the menu into her hand. "Don't spoil it when I'm trying to make up for my earlier boorishness. I want you to see that I don't have even generic pork chops on the menu. Go ahead. Look."

She opened the menu.

"Between the steak section and the chicken section."

"Right." She scanned the page and gasped. "Dean!"

There right in the middle, boxed in with golden scrollwork, was a picture of a mouthwatering pair of pork chops. The caption read: *Magnolia Harbor Inn Pork Chops, created by Magnolia Harbor Inn's co-owner, best-selling author and gourmet chef, Charlotte Wylde.*

He was watching her, obviously eager for her reaction.

"That's only a proof," he said quickly. "We haven't had them printed up yet. I can have that part removed if you think it's weird. I don't have to serve pork chops at all." He gave her a crooked little smile. "I only wanted to do something that would let people know those are your amazing creation."

"I don't know what to say," she admitted. "It's very sweet of you, but I don't want you to feel obligated—"

"I don't feel obligated. I wanted to right a wrong I did, and this is the best way I know to do it."

"But isn't that a conflict of interest for The Tidewater? Especially your restaurant."

"I don't think so. You don't serve dinner anyway, and why shouldn't people be able to try your pork chops? They're one of the best things on my menu, and my customers rave about them."

"Now you're being silly." She didn't know why she felt warmth creeping up her neck. Why did Dean keep it so hot in his office?

"No I'm not. They're wonderful." There was a twinkle in his eye.

"I wouldn't have 'borrowed' them if they weren't."

"Dean."

"Seriously," he said, "I think it's a good thing for both of us. We have happy dinner guests—guests you wouldn't be able to serve anyway—and you get a free ad for your cookbooks and your inn. Win-win, right?"

"I can't think of any reason it wouldn't be. As long as you're sure you don't mind. You don't have to do anything at all, especially now that we've cleared the air."

"I don't have to," he told her, taking hold of the menu. "I want to."

She didn't release her hold. "Okay, but only on one condition."

He raised his eyebrows. "What's that?"

"I get the first copy when you have them printed so that I have one on hand when I tell my guests to come here for dinner."

"Absolutely."

She let go of the menu, and he put it on his desk.

"I really do have to get back now," she said, fishing her keys out of her purse. "Thanks for standing with me about Laurie."

"I was glad to let her know she couldn't keep lying about you," he said. "Or me. And, to be honest, I've been wanting to straighten things out with you for a long time, but I was too much of a coward to take the first step."

"I didn't make it any easier for you, coming over here and accusing you of everything but eating that first apple."

He laughed. "I'm glad you didn't take it quite that far."

He escorted her to her car and waved as she drove away.

28

Grace

"Here, let me help you with that."

Grace hurried over to the stairs as Madison came down with her luggage.

"It's okay," Madison said. "I have a lot less to carry around than I did when I came here."

Grace couldn't help smiling. It was nice to see the peace in Madison's expression.

Madison followed her over to the front desk and put down her bags. "I wanted to thank you before anyone else comes down. I don't know who came up with that hatbox idea, but I'm glad it was here."

"It's our tradition," Grace told her as she totaled her bill and ran her credit card. "Who knows what God will use to help us through our hard times? Sometimes it's the simplest, most unlikely thing."

Madison nodded, looking a little shy. "I'm glad I ended up here. Your inn was exactly what I needed." She smiled and knelt down to give Winston a hug when he came from behind the desk with a little yip. "And so were you. Thank you for letting me play with you."

He licked her face, and she pressed a kiss to the top of his head.

"I thought Donny would be coming down too," Grace said, handing her back her card and her receipt when she stood up again. "He seems very nice."

Madison colored a little. "He is. And I found out we live only about twenty miles away from each other." She shrugged. "I don't know if that means anything, but we're going to keep each other company on the drive back, at least stopping along the way at the same time. We'll probably have lunch and dinner together. I'm enjoying getting to know him."

"If nothing else, you have a new friend. There's nothing wrong with that."

"Nothing wrong with what?" a low voice said, and now Madison really blushed.

"Donny." She smiled at him. "I was telling Grace there's nothing wrong with new friends getting to know each other better."

"I think it's a great idea," he said, handing his credit card to Grace without taking his eyes off Madison. "But we need to get a move on. I got a call earlier to sit in on a gig tonight at one of the clubs."

"Okay." There was a note of disappointment in Madison's voice. "Um, I've already checked out, so I'm ready when you are."

Grace handed Donny his credit card and receipt. "It's been very nice having you. We hope to see both of you again."

"You have a great place here," he said. "I'll be back whenever I can."

He put his bag over his shoulder and then picked up his suitcase. Then he picked up Madison's suitcase and carry-on.

"You don't have to do that," she said. "I know you're in a hurry."

"I'm never in too much of a hurry to be a gentleman." He nodded at Grace. "Thanks for everything."

"Thank you," Madison added, and they both headed toward the front door.

"Oh, I meant to tell you," Donny said as they walked out onto the front porch. "I can bring a guest to my gigs. If I remember right, you like jazz . . ."

Grace couldn't hear Madison's reply, but she could see the smile on her face. That was all she needed to see.

"Are they already gone?" Charlotte asked, drying her hands on a dish towel as she came out of the kitchen. "Were they doing okay?"

"More than okay I think," Grace told her. "So, with Keith and Mike well on their way, that only leaves Sarah in the honeymoon suite."

"Hopefully it's actually a honeymoon this time," Charlotte said with a grin.

"I think it's definite. Aidan had me look up the address of the justice of the peace and give him detailed directions on how to get there. So tomorrow we'll be able to register Mr. and Mrs. Nicholson for a six-night stay in the Dogwood Suite. At last."

"Wonderful." Charlotte's eyes shone. "We ought to make them a fabulous wedding breakfast before they go to the JP. I have a crab cake Benedict recipe I've been dying to try."

"I'm sure they'd love that. We'll ask them when they get back in, though I doubt either of them will be very interested in food the next few days."

Charlotte stifled a giggle as the bell over the front door rang.

"You won't believe it," Sarah said, her dark eyes wide. She clutched a large box against her.

"What happened?" Grace asked. "Where's Aidan?"

The glow on her face got brighter at the mention of his name. "He went to change for dinner, and I had to get this up to my room before he saw it."

She put the box on the front desk and lifted off the lid. Then, carefully removing the tissue paper that protected it, she lifted out a lovely vintage dress. It was tea-length with a full skirt, the pink silk only slightly faded, but otherwise in perfect condition. Grace guessed it had been made in the 1940s or '50s.

"Isn't it beautiful?" She held it up against herself. "It's almost exactly like the one my grandmother got married in. I've seen the pictures. I couldn't believe I found it and it's exactly my size. It's like it was meant to be mine."

Grace nodded. "I'm sure it was."

She was sure this was nothing like the designer dress Sarah must have chosen for her wedding extravaganza, but it was exactly right for a quiet ceremony at the justice of the peace. She found herself wishing she could be there to see it.

Sarah rummaged in the tissue paper and brought out a pair of ballet flats with matching wide ribbons in the same pale pink. "Shoes too. Aren't they precious?"

"So cute!" Charlotte took one from her. "That's amazing. Right on time too."

"The right time," Grace said.

The bell over the front door rang again, and Sarah scrambled to put the shoes and the dress back into the box as Aidan came in.

He smiled and shook his head. "How is it that I managed to get changed and get all the way back over here before you even got upstairs?"

"Something you'll find out tomorrow," Sarah said with a sly smile.

"Fair enough." He kissed the top of her head. "Still want to go out to dinner?"

"Yep. I'll be right back down." She grabbed the box and dashed up the stairs.

"I'm glad she's still excited about getting married," he said with a chuckle, "even if a no-frills JP ceremony isn't what she always wanted."

"I think you're what she's always wanted," Grace said. "She just had to realize it."

He ducked his head a little, his grin broadening. "I'm sorry none of her friends or family will be here."

"They'll understand," Charlotte said. "I think they'll be happy you two ended up married after all."

"Yeah." He glanced up the stairs. "You know, we talked about this a little bit, but she didn't want to impose on you. Still, it would be nice to have the two of you there. At the ceremony, I mean. As witnesses. And friends too."

"It is so kind of you to ask us. It might be hard for both of us to get away at the same time on such short notice," Grace told him, "but we will see what we can do."

"Grace should definitely go," Charlotte added quickly. "I can handle things here by myself for an hour or two, and she was the one who made you a sandwich and everything."

That made him laugh. "True. If it hadn't been for Grace, we might never have gotten back together."

"I don't know about that," Grace said.

"I do." Sarah pattered back down the stairs, fresh and beaming in white capri pants and a lacy white top. "Aidan, did you ask them?"

Aidan nodded. "They're not sure if they can both go, but I'm hoping Grace will say yes."

"Of course," Grace said, "but won't you need two witnesses? If Charlotte can't get away . . ."

"They'll have someone there, won't they?" Aidan said, suddenly unsure.

Sarah reached up to touch the butterfly pin that was still in her floppy hat. "Do you think your aunt would come? I know it's short notice, but she's been so sweet to both of us. It would be perfect."

"I can't think of anybody—other than Charlotte—that I'd rather have," Aidan added.

"All right," Grace said. "I'll give her a call and see if she can come, but I'm sure she wouldn't miss it. We'll check with her and let you know over hors d'oeuvres tonight. For now, you two enjoy your evening and don't worry about tomorrow. I'm sure you'll have the most beautiful wedding ever."

"I know we will." Sarah stood on her tiptoes and kissed Aidan's cheek. "I just know it."

"We'll see you later," Aidan said, and hand in hand he and Sarah went out the front door.

"There." Charlotte nodded toward the door. "I don't know how you can say nobody ever listens to your advice."

Grace laughed softly. "Maybe they listen, but they don't usually follow it."

"It worked out all the same, didn't it?"

"Yeah, I guess it did. Even for you."

"Even for me." Charlotte shook her head. "Who would have thought Dean could be so nice about everything?"

"Including the pork chops."

Charlotte grinned. "Including the pork chops, though you and Aunt Winnie could have been a little less smug when I told you about it all at lunch."

"Well, we did tell you so." Grace slung an arm around her shoulders. "What good is it to be a big sister if you can't be right once in a while?"

"I'm glad you are," Charlotte said, twisting to hug her in return.

The bell over the front door rang, and the sisters looked at each other.

"That'll be Bluebell, I suppose," Charlotte said.

"Or Rosebud. They're due in about now." Grace went to greet the newcomers with a smile. "Welcome to Magnolia Harbor Inn. We hope your stay will be a happy and peaceful one."

Learn more about Annie's fiction books at

AnniesFiction.com

We've designed the Annie's Fiction website especially for you!

Access your e-books • Read sample chapters • Manage your account

Choose from one of these great series:

Amish Inn Mysteries
Annie's Attic Mysteries
Annie's Mysteries Unraveled
Annie's Quilted Mysteries
Annie's Secrets of the Quilt
Antique Shop Mysteries
Chocolate Shoppe Mysteries
Creative Woman Mysteries
Hearts of Amish Country
Secrets of the Castleton Manor Library
Victorian Mansion Flower Shop Mysteries

What are you waiting for? Visit us now at **AnniesFiction.com!**

Victorian Mansion Flower Shop Mysteries™

Set on sparkling Puget Sound in the cozy island town of Turtle Cove, Washington, the stories in this enthralling series are good old-fashioned whodunits chock-full of fascinating family secrets, breathtaking scenery, heartwarming discoveries, and the unbreakable bonds of female friendships.

If you love the great outdoors, gardens, birds, flowers, and a good mystery book . . . then you'll love Annie's *Victorian Mansion Flower Shop Mysteries*!

AnniesFiction.com